SOME MUST DIE

This is a tale of love, terror and heroism set against the background of a Central American revolution; of an English schoolgirl who flowers to passionate womanhood while the Republic of Havamo erupts in civil war; and of the cold, self-sacrificing courage of a newspaper editor who believes himself a coward. The basic theme is the perennial and apparently hopeless struggle of the underdog against oppression.

LAURENCE MOODY

SOME MUST DIE

Complete and Unabridged

LINFORD
Leicester

First published in Great Britain in 1964 by
Robert Hale Limited
London

First Linford Edition
published 2004
by arrangement with
Robert Hale Limited
London

British Library CIP Data

Moody, Laurence
Some must die.—Large print ed.—
Linford mystery library
1. Suspense fiction
2. Large type books
I. Title
823.9′14 [F]

ISBN 1–84395–575–X

Published by
F. A. Thorpe (Publishing)
Anstey, Leicestershire

Set by Words & Graphics Ltd.
Anstey, Leicestershire
Printed and bound in Great Britain by
T. J. International Ltd., Padstow, Cornwall

This book is printed on acid-free paper

To
AUDREY

'In these adjustments it hath always been that some must die for the benefit and improvement of the greater number; some will perish of necessity, some uselessly by mischance, but one there must be who for example's sake will play the martyr.'

Hernando Cortez

1

The offices of *Verdad* sit on one side of an immense square called the Plaza Mayor, on top of the only hill in Real Barba, capital of the Republic of Havamo.

From the editor's window the whole of the Old Town and vast expanses of the yellow hinterland are visible on clear days. This height gave to the newspaper's offices a fictitious semblance of dominance which irked Barrett, the editor.

In the days when his wife was alive Barrett had helped to mould public opinion in an area measuring some fourteen or fifteen thousand square miles.

Today he sat staring at a sheet of paper on his desk. It was headed *Policy Directive* and at its foot were stamped the words *Office of Escobar*.

The moulding of public opinion was now taken care of elsewhere.

Martyn Barrett was one of the few Englishmen left in Real Barba. He thought it likely that soon he would be the only one.

He was a large middle-aged man of clumsy build, with sandy-grey hair rapidly thinning. He looked easy-going but that was deceptive. There were dark patches of perspiration at the armpits of his shirt, which he changed three times a day. He smoked Durango cigars practically continuously from the moment he left his bed every morning in his flat on the edge of the Everglades until he returned to it early the following morning.

When in the mood he was wont to talk well and persuasively; these days he talked less than formerly but swore more frequently.

From the newspaper he derived a considerable income but apart from that he no longer had any tangible ties on the Isthmus.

His daughter was safe at finishing school in England (he still thought of England in terms of his own youth). There could not now be any immediate prospect of her visiting him, much as he had looked forward to seeing her again.

By now he had reconciled himself to that hard necessity.

He rose heavily and went to the open window and stared out.

To the south-west lay the *ganaderias* where the black fighting bulls were reared. Here and there mottled patches marked the meagre farms of the *peons*. The buildings were low and flat and mostly of adobe, except for the substantial masses of the cathedral and the circular arena — from his hilltop Barrett could glimpse the red *barrera* surrounding the yellow coin of sand.

The entrance to the plaza had two square sandstone towers with tin roofs on which he could just make out a couple of vultures, heads sunk into shoulders. They kept giving peevish flaps and lifting their clawed feet alternately to cool them from the heat of the roof. At that distance they resembled bald asthmatic old men with low foreheads and big hooked noses.

It was a scorched land, hard and poor, yet to Barrett it seemed that if any dignity and virtue were left in the isthmus, it lingered there.

He brought his gaze back to the New Town, to the other side of the Plaza Mayor a third of a mile away, where the sun glinted on fast-moving Cadillacs and a couple of skyscrapers reared, managing even to dwarf the massive barracks of the Army alongside.

Beyond the skyscrapers he could see the derricks of the oil wells recently confiscated from their foreign owners and now as impotent as a painted backcloth.

The skyscrapers, the barracks and the enlargement of the square to its present gigantic size were all new since the coming of Escobar. Every time he stood there and looked out the contrast between old and new seemed more startling.

He spat suddenly on the parapet outside his window and the spittle made a sizzling sound and instantly dried on the hot concrete.

At first, he recalled, the new order had seemed a good thing; then, not so long ago, at least tolerable.

He, a journalist, should have known better — he at least should have recognised the Gadarene slope, distrusted the gentle incline at the beginning.

His eyes were drawn back to the *ganaderias* again. The people down there, outside the town, were by tradition *peons*, under-dogs, yet once or twice in the past they had for a brief space become wolves. Some day, he tried to persuade himself, the under-dogs would whelp a few more wolves.

When that day came he would very much like to be a wolf himself but his courage, he told himself ruefully, was not of that order.

He went back to his desk and tore the sheet of paper across, then looked over his shoulder quickly to make sure no one else was in the room. He did this every week. One day, he promised himself wistfully and without conviction, he would not only make the gesture of tearing up the directive. He would disregard its contents.

After all, his daughter was safe in England . . .

Looking inwards after the bright sunlight of the window it took him several moments to register the fact that this time there really was someone else in the room behind him.

And several more to realise the someone was his daughter. A cold prickle of sweat ran over his body.

'Judie!' he exclaimed. 'Well, for God's sake — Judie!'

She came over and put her arms round his neck and reached up to kiss him. Although they had seen so little of each other there had always been a deep affection between them, perhaps all the deeper for being undemonstrative.

Of a sudden he felt absurdly happy in spite of the anxiety underneath — he had not seen her for four years, a longer interval than ever before.

'God in heaven,' he said, 'you've grown up.'

He held her at arms length to examine her, fair-haired and pretty and certainly not any longer a schoolgirl. Her lipstick — surely that was new. And there were curves where before there had been flatness. 'All this equipment — where did it come from?'

She laughed. 'It just growed.'

'You're twenty. That's it — I've been picturing you as still sixteen. But — why did you come — ?'

She hesitated, nibbling her lip in a nervous little mannerism he remembered from her childhood.

'Because you told me not to, I'm afraid. I didn't dare let you know I was on my way — you'd only have sent me back, wouldn't you?'

He said seriously, 'I most certainly would. Things aren't too good here. And liable to get worse.'

'Then you'll need someone to look after you. And I simply don't believe the people out there are energetic enough to start fighting each other, if that's what you mean. They're all asleep with hats over their eyes.'

'Siesta,' he explained. 'You must have come through the Old Town.'

She eyed him uncertainly.

'Well — aren't you glad to see me?'

'You know I'm glad.' He stood irresolutely for a moment, then began to put on his linen jacket and grinned at her.

'But you'll just have to give me a minute or two to recover.' He spread his arms and let them fall again. 'Well, young lady — what do we do next?'

'There's a taxi at the door — could you pay him off, please?' she said. 'Then we've got a lot to talk about so you can take me to a coffee bar. Or do they have coffee bars here?'

He grinned again.

'We'll go to Paco's.'

As they went down in the passenger-controlled elevator Judie said, 'I'm going to call you Martyn — is that all right? The girls at school all did it.'

For a fleeting moment he was a little taken aback. There are juke-boxes in Real Barba and the young people have long since learned American ways but they do not address their parents by their Christian names.

Martyn Barrett looked at his daughter's face and suddenly realised that behind this soignée young woman hid a child who had made a long, lonely and rather frightening journey to be with him, but whose doubts about the wisdom of it all were at this moment as great as his own.

'Now there's a coincidence,' he said. 'I was just going to suggest that very thing myself.'

She reached up and kissed him again quickly.

At street level the heat was oppressive. Barrett's car was parked in the yard at the back of the building but he knew from long experience that the effort of driving the short distance to Paco's would bathe him in sweat again.

They got into the waiting taxi and swung out of the Plaza Mayor down towards the Plaza del Castillo and the adobe buildings.

A thin line of orange trees fringed this smaller, older square; between them was strung an electric cable carrying coloured bulbs. In the centre stood a statue of El Bombita, the most famous *torero* Real Barba had ever produced, killed a decade ago in the local ring.

A man in a huge sombrero was sprinkling the surface of the square but the water seemed to disappear almost as soon as it hit the caked soil.

Away beyond the white buildings lay the Everglades and somewhere beyond them again was the Gulf, seldom visible because of the heat haze though sometimes at night the haze lifted and then from his flat Barrett could see the moon shining far out on the water.

He paid off the taxi and they went under the awning of Paco's and sat on wicker chairs and ordered coffee.

Out in the square a few pigeons were strutting about, pecking at invisible things in the cracks. The light was so strong that everything looked either white or black, except for the ground which was sienna. On a wall nearby a gaudy poster showed a matador doing an incredibly statuesque *pase de la muerte*.

There were only a few people round the square, drowsing over drinks in the shade of the arcades.

Barrett wondered uneasily what sort of impression it was making on Judie. Probably unfavourable. He must bring her down again around midnight when the late *paseo* was on and things were livelier.

'Well,' he said. 'tell me about it. How did you come?'

'By plane,' she told him.

'That's pretty expensive.'

'I know. Most of it I saved from your allowance — I must say you were awfully generous, Martyn. The rest I borrowed from Aunt Bertha. Without telling her what it was for, of course.'

'I'll bet,' he said, remembering his sister. 'I'll send her a cheque.'

Sitting there over his coffee he began to do some hard thinking, to try to plan at this late hour a way of life for them both that should have been planned long since.

Twenty-five years ago, soon after his marriage, he had come to the newspaper as English correspondent. The opportunity had been fortuitous and they had accepted it as such, never dreaming for a moment that it would last more than a year or two.

But things had continued to run his way. The language had come easily to him, he had found himself in sympathy with the liberal policy of the paper and its attitude to local conditions. Soon Real

Barba accepted him and valued his opinion.

When the editor had died Barrett had jumped at the unexpected offer of the vacant editorial chair.

Then, shortly after the birth of Judie, her mother had died too. In despair at her loss and unable to face rearing the child by himself in Real Barba, he had taken her back to England and left her in charge of his sister Bertha. He had provided for her schooling and upbringing and had then returned to his editorship because that was the only shred of the old good life left.

Every few years he had taken a couple of months off and visited Judie and they had spent a holiday together in England or the Continent happily getting to know each other again.

There had always been a tacit understanding that at some unspecified future time she would rejoin him in Real Barba.

Then had come the revolution.

Because of the changes it had brought and might yet bring he had kept postponing Judie's return. And now Judie had taken the matter into her own hands.

'You're cross, aren't you, Martyn?' she said in a small voice, breaking the silence. 'You don't really want me here, do you?'

He looked at her and was horrified to see tears in her eyes. He took her hand in his and held it shyly for a moment.

He said awkwardly, 'I've wanted you here more than anything else on earth — please believe that, Judie. I kept putting it off because — well, Real Barba won't be too healthy a place for people we love if there's a counter revolution.'

She brightened visibly at his clumsy sincerity. And suddenly she laughed.

'But look at it! It's fascinating, in a way it's even beautiful — but it's asleep. I just can't imagine the tumbrils rolling through this town — '

He let go her hand and lit a cigar. He was remembering the torn directive lying on his desk.

'Well,' he said, 'well — I don't know. I suppose I could be wrong — maybe things *could* get better as well as worse.'

'This man — Escobar, isn't it? — I suppose he's a dictator. But the man before him was a dictator too, wasn't he? So why should it make all that difference, Martyn?'

Before replying Barrett glanced over his shoulder casually. Miguel the waiter was lolling against the counter inside, well out of earshot. Barrett had nothing against Miguel; it was just another sign of the times, he reflected, that the small precaution should seem natural.

'At least Merida was popular,' he said, keeping his voice low. 'If there'd been an election he'd still have got in. He made mistakes, of course. But the people knew that their happiness and prosperity were his first concern. Besides, he didn't have an overwhelming instrument at hand to enforce his rule if the people got tired of it. Escobar has. No matter how sick of him the people get they can't do a thing about it — not so long as the Army sticks by him. And he's taking damn good care the Army does just that, by methods most decent people would condemn. That's the difference. It's a set-up as old as time. But it's still a hell of a difference.'

Judie puckered her brow.

'But if he were to do anything really stinking — a massacre or something like that — surely one of the big Powers would intervene?'

Barrett shook his head.

'Nope, they're too busy watching each other. Anyway they've learned that poking their noses into the domestic affairs of small countries doesn't pay off any more. No — if there's a counter rising here it'll have to be organised and carried through by the people themselves.' He nodded towards the man in the sombrero sprinkling the square. 'By people like him. They won't have a chance. What would he fight with — that ruddy sprinkler? But if and when the time comes, that won't stop him and others like him from trying.'

Judie nodded soberly. She was silent for a moment, then she said, 'My — my luggage is at the airport. I wasn't sure . . . '

Of a sudden Barrett was immensely happy again. For a moment General Escobar might not have existed. There was just his daughter who had crossed an ocean to be with him.

He said, 'Let's return to the office and I'll tell Tom — that's young Tom Clark my assistant editor — I'm taking the rest of the day off. You must meet him and Tio and all the others some time — let 'em see the old man's capable of producing something else besides a newspaper. But right now first thing we'll go back and get out the car and collect your stuff and take it to the flat. You were born there, honey — not actually in the present flat, that's new, but they built it on the same site.'

It was still too hot to walk back up the hill. Barrett called to the waiter, 'Miguel, get me a taxi, will you?'

He left a coin on the table. They rose and she slipped an arm through his. 'Oh hell,' he said happily, 'it's good to be a family man again . . .'

When, nearly two hours later, they got to the flat, Judie was drawn to it at once.

Maria, Barrett's elderly housekeeper, accepted her new charge as she accepted everything — with complete equanimity. Merida's going and Escobar's coming had caused not a ripple on the surface of

Maria's philosophy. Such things were decided on some other plane of existence, along with death and earthquakes and the process of growing old. Some were bad, like being old and fat and ugly, which she felt herself to be; some good, like the arrival of Senor Barrett's daughter. None had she any power to change — except possibly the fatness — so why make oneself miserable worrying about them?

Barrett took Judie up to the first-floor bedroom which was to be hers. It looked out across the tangled Everglades towards the invisible Gulf. An ochre-tinged sun hung low in the brazen sky like the yolk of an egg. She stared out in silence for a long time and then turned and buried her face in his shoulder and cried like a puppy that has lost its mother.

'Here,' he exclaimed helplessly, 'hold on — for goodness' sake — '

She looked up at him and dried her eyes.

'It's going to work out,' she said. 'Oh Martyn — it's going to be all right. Aunt Bertha did her best — but I meant nothing to her. Now I've come home . . . '

* * *

One thing surprised Barrett. In the course of their first conversation with Maria he discovered that Judie's Spanish was almost as good as his own. Evidently those school fees hadn't been wasted.

A little before midnight they drove down again to the Plaza del Castillo. It no longer slumbered. The lights between the orange trees had been switched on and crowds of people were strolling about the square past the crowded tables, eternally round and round in the velvet night, some few occasionally pausing to buy a drink.

It always amused Barrett to observe how the young men and women in this *paseo* mixed but little yet were intensely aware of each other, the men making no secret of their interest, the girls pretending complete indifference. It reminded him of the mating displays of birds he sometimes watched on the fringe of the Everglades. Only here it was the female who wore the more gorgeous plumage; no matter how poor the family it was a point of honour that the daughter of the house should issue forth to the *paseo* in freshly-ironed frock of dazzling white or vivid colour over a flare of frilly petticoats.

It was only here in the centuries-old Plaza del Castillo that the *paseo* was held. The Plaza Mayor was too big, too new, too impersonal; something about it seemed unfriendly to tradition.

Paco's was full but Barrett found a vacant table at the Faena.

He ordered a whisky for himself and a sherry for Judie and glanced around. When there were bullfighters in town this was the cafe they frequented but tonight there did not seem to be any of the fraternity present. It pleased him to notice that Judie was coming in for her full share of the male admiration; blondes are a novelty in Real Barba.

Then he had a spasm of anxiety again. The sheltered life of a girls' finishing school — as he imagined it — could scarcely be an adequate preparation for life here on the isthmus.

He lit a cigar and eyed her covertly and observed with some surprise that her face presented the same mask of indifference as did those of the girls in the *paseo*. He thought, I really must remember she's twenty and knows the rules of the sisterhood.

'Well, honey, what do you think of it?' he prompted.

She turned towards him and the mask slipped a bit and he saw she was happy and thrilled and enjoying herself immensely.

'That thing we were talking about — it can't happen here, it just can't,' she said. She chuckled. 'The people out there aren't thinking about anything like that. They're thinking about making love. And of nothing else — every blessed one of them. Can't you feel it, Martyn — ?'

He grinned. That was something the school hadn't taught her either — but she was right. From somewhere up in the New Town his ear caught the sound of a jeep starting up and the insignificant impression was pigeonholed in his mind.

'Maybe — for the moment,' he acknowledged. 'But they can change faster than you could wink.'

As Barrett finished his drink he could hear the sound of the jeep coming down the hill. He wondered why he should bother to listen to it through the chatter of the *paseo*.

He put his glass down and the jeep drove into the centre of the square and stopped.

There were four soldiers in it dressed in the familiar olive-green uniform. They kept the engine running while two of them got out and walked to opposite sides of the square. Each nailed a notice to an orange tree, then walked quickly back to the jeep and jumped in.

The jeep turned sharply, scattering the yellow dust, and accelerated out of the square back towards the New Town.

Nobody in the Plaza del Castillo paid the slightest attention to the jeep (except to get out of its way) or looked towards the notices.

But somehow the chatter had taken on a different note, it was a little lower now and sounded less spontaneous.

Judie said curiously, 'What's happened, Martyn?'

‘It’s like I said,’ he told her. ‘They can change quickly. They’re not thinking about making love any more.’

She sat in silence for a moment. The *paseo* continued to go round and round like a wheel rotating on its axis, the hub of which was the statue of El Bombita. Instead of getting cooler the night seemed more oppressively hot than ever.

Presently she said, ‘It’s the notices, isn’t it? Why don’t the people go over and read them?’

He took a long pull at his cigar.

‘When you want to show dislike or contempt of anything there are several ways you can do it. One of the best is to ignore it.’

‘Is there something terrible in the notices?’

‘Shouldn’t think so — probably just another slight turn of the screw. It’s only at the end when the screw gets really tight that it becomes terrible. We’ve got quite a bit to go yet. Now let’s get into that *paseo* and give the boys a break.’

Judie chuckled as they rose.

‘Come on, wolves,’ she murmured,

'don't let me down. Get those whistles working . . . '

When, a little later, they were driving back to the flat, Judie said sleepily, 'I caught a glimpse of one of those notices as we passed. Didn't seem to be worth getting excited about — just something headed 'New Agrarian Laws' . . . '

* * *

It took a day for the purport of the new laws to spread through the countryside beyond the Old Town.

Nobody thought they would make much difference. When you and your father and your father's father have lived in a certain way it is difficult to believe that sticking a piece of paper on a tree will alter things all that much.

Nearly all the families owned the patches of land on which they worked. In some cases they even boasted that ownership had passed down from father to son since the time of the Conquistadors. Among themselves the people referred to these patches of land as farms and to each other as farmers. Both terms were misnomers. In actual fact they were *peons* scratching a bare living from dried-up scrub. But in their own eyes they were *hacendados*, landowners.

The owners of the *ganaderias* on which the fighting bulls were reared were in a somewhat different category. There were only four or five of them in all but they really were people of some substance. A *ganaderia* is a tract of grassland with wooded areas, a water supply and certain technical offices. Even if the grassland is not of top quality it is, just the same, a not contemptible possession.

These were the two classes most affected by the new agrarian laws which laid down that in future all agricultural land would be regarded as technically belonging to the State, and went on to explain that this would not immediately entail any drastic change provided one quarter of the profit on all such land were handed over to the said State.

The reason for this new arrangement, it was added, was the necessity to put the finances for the upkeep of the

Army, which was the guardian and protector of the people's rights, on a sound footing.

None of this was very original. At the foot were the words *Office of Escobar*.

The reaction of the people was in no way original either.

Don Luis Ribera, who owned the biggest of the *ganaderias* and whose *divisa* on bulls ensured good attendances even in the plazas away across the border and up in Mexico City itself, invited his fellow breeders to dinner and discussed with them the implications of the new measure. No action was decided upon. It was agreed it would be best to wait and see if the hare jumped again and if so, how far.

The farmers did not even get so far as this. For one thing they were not in the habit of giving dinner parties. And for another, they had already read in the paper *Verdad* (those of them who could read) that 'the new Agrarian Laws will, of course, be loyally accepted as necessary for the security of the State and the happiness of the people'.

Probably none of the farmers knew that such things as policy directives existed.

* * *

A few days later Don Luis Ribera, meeting Barrett in the street, suggested it might amuse his daughter to ride over the Ribera ranch. It was arranged that Barrett would take Judie out the following afternoon.

The Ribera *estancia* was not what it had once been. In the old days it had made handsome profits but now it was run on a shoestring. On one thing only was Don Luis adamant — the quality of his bulls must not be allowed to deteriorate. Provided that were achieved he was content to break even at the end of every year — break even and continue to live in a faded semblance of the old style.

But to Judie it proved an enchantment, faded or not.

After cocktails — presided over by Dona Vittoria the ranchero's wife — the men and their visitors rode out through the creeper-covered archway on to the sweeping pasture.

The dome of the sky seemed vaster here than in England. To the south a powder-blue line of mountains was painted on the horizon; even at that distance the sun picked out a needle of white on one of the summits, the Christ of Tlazcala.

The eight horses moved delicately, alertly over the pastures, silent except for the creaking of their leathers. Four servants with steel-tipped *varas* led the cavalcade, then came Don Luis with Barrett riding clumsily alongside. Judie, looking the part in jodhpurs, brought up the rear with Ribera's son Juan in attendance.

He was a good-looking youth this Juan, very brown and as lithe as a matador in his first season. When they were introduced Judie had addressed him in Spanish but he had replied in perfect English with a slight American accent; he had, in fact, been educated at a Californian university.

At the far end of the immense pasture was a cluster of poplars and in their shadow stood the steel-black fighting bulls, their heads lifting as they watched the approaching horses with, as yet, only curiosity.

The four *vaqueros* spread out in front like a screen. The bulls were still a good way off when Don Luis held up his hand.

'Near enough, I think,' he said.

The eight horses froze like statues. One of the bulls trotted a few yards out from the shadow of the trees into the hot sunlight and stood searching for movement in his line of vision. Judie could hear him snorting softly through his nostrils. Behind the deadly horns she saw the neck muscle rising.

'He is coming,' Don Luis said softly. 'Carlos, move out.'

The *vaquero* on the left of the screen wheeled his horse and moved quietly away from the party. He kept his eyes glued on the bull, controlling the horse with the pressure of his knees. He called gently, '*Huy, toro!*' And again, '*Huy, toro!*' At the same time he turned the horse away, watching the bull over his shoulder, his *vara* trailing loosely in his right hand.

Suddenly the bull charged like a thunderbolt. He came as levelly as a train on rails and almost with as much striking power. With the reflex speed of a released spring the horse was away, his tail swishing excitedly. For perhaps twenty yards the horns crept nearer the sleek flanks, then the horse began to draw away with every stride.

Having demonstrated his authority the bull dug in his forefeet and brought his lethal half-ton of bone and muscle to a prancing, snorting stop.

Don Luis chuckled.

'Let's go elsewhere,' he said. 'The flies are troubling them. Carlos will keep the bulls' attention distracted from us.'

As they moved away Juan eyed the girl riding beside him and noted the eager unsatisfied excitement in her blue eyes.

'Some day,' he said, 'you must let me take you to a *corrida. La senorita* es *aficionada* — I can see it in her face.'

'The senorita is scared to death,' she told him, laughing.

Don Luis and Barrett, riding behind now and out of hearing, were already talking of other things.

'If it is not an impertinence to ask,' Don Luis remarked with careful carelessness. 'That paragraph in your paper approving these new agrarian laws . . . the sentiments, perhaps, were not yours, Senor Barrett — ?'

A slow flush spread over the editor's features.

'Well, now,' he temporised, 'which paragraph was that? It may have been contributed — it's a rule in our business, you know, that contributed matter needn't necessarily reflect the editor's opinion. However, let's not talk shop — '

But the casual visit had suddenly been given point. Don Luis was already establishing who was friend and who foe in the coming struggle — and Barrett had dodged the issue.

As they rode round the *ganaderia* the editor squirmed uncomfortably in his saddle. A man without courage, he reflected bitterly, is like a woman without virtue . . .

⋆ ⋆ ⋆

On the outskirts of the City and in the neighbouring *pueblos* there presently began to be a new and more specific stir of uneasiness.

Officials from the New Town visited each farm in turn. They made an arbitrary assessment of the probable yearly profit to be derived from each scrap of land and divided it by four.

This fourth, they explained, represented the amount of Agrarian Tax payable to the State. Settlement could be made in cash and in kind.

To the farmers the assessment seemed so absurdly large, so palpably impossible to satisfy, that they made a joke of it. In the wineshops there was much laughter, each farmer vying with his neighbour as to which had received the most enormous, the most ridiculous bill.

In the end it was accepted that General Escobar for some reason of propaganda best known to himself was merely staging a demonstration. Even the General couldn't alter the laws of arithmetic.

In the case of the *ganaderias*, which were also visited by the tax officials, the assessments were less arbitrary. Unlike the farmers the rancheros kept books and it was a simple matter to arrive at a figure. Nevertheless, were payment ever to be enforced the breeders would be ruined no less surely than the farmers, for none of the *ganaderias* was doing more than breaking even financially.

In the circumstances it is not to be wondered at that their owners, like their poorer neighbours, could not bring themselves to take the thing seriously.

Barrett sensed the deeper threat beneath, that failure to pay the assessed tax might offer an excuse to implement the other half of the decree — the confiscation of all land by the State.

He recognised that every man's interest in his land was theoretically short of being absolute, but he also knew that in practice the *peon's* plot was the one thing its cultivator felt sure about, the one possession that gave him substance, the only real reason he had for feeling proud of Havamo citizenship.

There have been many revolutions in Havamo since the time of Cortez but none that attempted to take the smallholding away from its immemorial owner. Barrett wondered if Escobar was going to be the first to have a shot at it.

As yet, however, the threat was only on paper. It was as if a breeze had crept through a forest. For a moment the leaves had shivered but soon they became inert again.

* * *

In his flat on the edge of the Everglades a new comfort, a new orderliness, had come into Barrett's life.

Faithful though Maria was he wondered how he had put up for so long with her ideas of housekeeping.

For the first time in almost twenty years his flat had become his home, thanks to Judie. He had held the common male belief that two women cannot share a kitchen amicably and was astonished when Maria and Judie remained on the best of terms.

He had introduced Judie to all the *Verdad* staff and now quite often took her with him to the office. Her shorthand and typing were adequate and came in useful but she made her presence felt in other ways too.

For instance little vases of flowers appeared on his desk — and Tom Clark began to comb his hair more carefully.

Tom had come as trainee to Barrett at the age of fifteen and now, almost ten years later, was assistant editor. He was the son of one of the English engineers at the oil wells. When the wells had been taken over by Escobar the Company had withdrawn its employees but Tom had stayed on in Real Barba.

During the past week the remaining members of the British Colony had packed up and gone away north, as Barrett had foreseen they would do. He and Judie and Tom Clark were now the only British residents left in town. Barrett, who — literally and metaphorically — had never had much time for the social round, did not feel the loss unduly. With Tom it was different; he missed the activities which the young people of the colony had formerly organised.

Now with the coming of Judie he was finding life rosier again.

Barrett took care that Escobar's policy directives were not now left lying about. But in a storeroom of the *Verdad* building there were dusty files of back numbers of the paper covering the fifty years of its existence; Judie took to dusting these and in the process perused their contents.

She found in them inconsistencies which puzzled her.

One night after supper she and Barrett were sitting on the balcony of the flat; a full moon like a Maya mask hung over the Everglades and the voices of frogs and cicadas filled the night. After a period of silence Judie asked casually, 'In Merida's time you printed what you liked, didn't you, Martyn — he didn't interfere?'

Barrett studied the end of his cigar. 'No,' he agreed, 'he didn't interfere. The press was free. I told you he was a good man.'

'But now,' she persisted gently, 'it's got to be what Escobar says, hasn't it? In important things, I mean. If it's unimportant you can still say what you like. But if it's about politics or taxes or things like that you've got to print what he tells you, isn't that right?'

A slow flush spread over Barrett's face; he took a long time about replying.

'Honey,' he said at last, 'sometimes a paper's got to speak for a while in a voice other than its own — or die. Escobar sends me a policy directive every week. Mostly it's only a line or two, sometimes a couple of paragraphs. I try to persuade myself such a little bit of a thing can't be important. There's a time to compromise — and maybe a time when compromise must have an end. I — I honestly don't think that time's arrived yet.'

'When it does arrive, Escobar's going to be awfully angry,' Judie said. 'That's why you didn't want me here, isn't it, Martyn?'

He shrugged.

'The time may never come. And even if it does I'm not sure I'd have the courage to do anything — except pack up and go. There'd probably be nothing else to do, nothing that would be any use.'

She was looking at him very seriously now. It came to him suddenly that to her he appeared a much finer person than he had ever appeared to himself.

'You'll do something all right,' she said. 'Just promise me one thing. When that time comes, Martyn, don't worry about me — do what you've got to do. I'd feel a heel if my being here interfered with that.'

He thought, her new responsibilities — looking after me, planning the household — have developed her; she's all woman now. He got up, stretched himself, stubbed out his cigar and grinned at her.

'Hell,' he said, 'I can't promise that — it's all too damned hypothetical, there are too many imponderables. Come on young lady, time for bed . . . '

⋆ ⋆ ⋆

On the fourth Sunday after Judie's arrival a *corrida* was announced in the Plaza of Real Barba — the last the city was to see for a long time.

Juan Ribera asked her to go with him; then an hour later Tom Clark also invited her. Judie explained about the prior invitation and Tom said, 'Oh Juan — I know him. Don't suppose he'd mind if I came too.'

She had her doubts about that but next day Tom sought her out and told her airily, 'By the way, I happened to run into Juan last night. He doesn't mind.'

So Judie was well and truly escorted to her first bull-fight.

Just inside the entrance to the Plaza Juan hired cushions and Tom bought paper visors. They sat far back in the upper *tendido* of *sombra*, which is the shady side. As the two men said, in the event of Judie disliking the *corrida* her dislike would be less away up there where the emphasis is on the pattern woven by man and bull more than on the technical mechanics whereby the matador strives to approach death as closely as possible without actually embracing it.

The amount of noise and colour packed into the Plaza was to Judie almost incredible.

Down below in the *callejon* encircling the ring attendants were opening sword cases, laying cerise and cherry capes across the *barrera*, eyeing pretty girls in the seats above. Around her everyone was talking, passing flasks, laughing, arguing, fanning themselves with programmes, pointing, calling to each other, adjusting cushions, standing up to wave, buying ice-creams from red-shirted vendors — or just waiting.

Across her Juan and Tom were exchanging acerbities, the beginning of which she had missed . . .

Juan was saying, 'But only an Englishman would forget that two's company, three's none — '

'Just what did you expect me to do?' Tom snapped back. 'Leave an innocent schoolgirl at the mercy of a lecherous Latin — ?'

She looked at them in panic and saw they were grinning from ear to ear; obviously they must know each other very well.

'Heavens,' she laughed, 'I thought I was coming to watch fighting bulls — not sit between them.'

Suddenly a trumpet blew and two horsemen dressed in the manner of sixteenth-century Spain were galloping towards her across the sand.

They paused, bowed, backed across the ring, rode forward again. Behind them now followed the parade of *toreros* — the whole panoply of the *corrida* — headed by the three swaggering matadors, the sun sparkling on the gold and silver lamé of their brocaded suits.

Almost before she realised it the circle of sand was empty again. She heard the crowd sigh and become silent. Everyone was staring at the gate of the *toril* over on the sunny side of the arena.

It opened and into the ring thundered the first bull of the afternoon.

Judie was lucky in her first bullfight. There was much of it she didn't understand — Juan and Tom chattered away about terrains and *querencias* and *remates*; and some which she disliked, particularly the *suerte* of the picadors. But the virtuosity of the banderilleros seemed to her astonishing and that of the matadors with the cape miraculous.

She remembered how, mounted on a swift and well-schooled horse on the ranch of Juan's father and with four *vaqueros* to protect her, she had felt how impossible it would be to survive the bull's attack in any way except flight.

Yet here before her a slim pygmy of a man, a Mexican gipsy, so dominated two bulls with a piece of cloth that at times she could have sworn the huge beasts were voluntarily performing a well-rehearsed and intricate dance round their human teacher, whose feet remained immobile while he guided his pupils through their steps solely with his arms. She was lucky in that the bulls that afternoon were brave and honest and Nicanor Giron brave and inspired.

When the matador came out to thunderous '*Olés!*' after his second bull, she saw with wonder that the lovely brocade of his *chaquetilla* was sliced and gashed by the horns and his own brown flesh showing through.

'Well,' Juan said, shrugging, 'you can't work much closer than that.'

‘He had good bulls,’ Tom said. ‘Not like those overgrown calves your father breeds and sells as *toros*.’

One man in superlative form can set a *corrida* alight so that the other *toreros* perform above themselves. Giron did it that afternoon in Real Barba — yet it was not because of him that the *corrida* was afterwards remembered.

It is traditional on the isthmus for the crowd to stand up and cheer the president as he leaves his box (the president of the *corrida* is some high local personage who acts as a sort of honorary umpire for the afternoon). Judie could not see the president because his box was below and to one side of her and surrounded by a wooden partition, but she guessed he was leaving when the people stood up.

She and Juan and Tom stood also and waited for the cheering and the *Olés*, which had been vociferous when the bullfighters were leaving the ring, to break out again. Instead there was silence.

She saw Juan and Tom glance at each other quickly. Then in the cheap seats on the far side someone whistled insultingly.

This whistle was immediately backed up by another — and another and another. In an instant the arena was swept by a gale of mass venom.

The commonplace demonstration was made significant by the fact that there had been no lead-up to it such as cowardice or inept work by a *torero*. Judie was puzzled and a little startled. It took her a moment to realise the disapproval was directed towards the president's box.

Then suddenly the infection spread to the expensive seats of *sombra*. A man immediately in front of Judie jumped to his feet with an imprecation and hurled his leather cushion at the box. His face was that of a wild beast.

In a trice the air was filled with flying cushions and enraged shouts. She saw a bottle smash against the wooden partition. Men in olive-green uniforms with drawn batons began to form a cordon round the box.

And then the thing was over as quickly as it had begun, the threat and ugliness gone out of it as the last of the air goes from a pricked balloon.

The crowd began to file quietly out of the Plaza.

'Good heavens,' Judie exclaimed, 'what did the president do to deserve that — who is he, anyway?'

'Oh him — General Escobar,' Tom said. 'I thought you knew.' He was silent for a moment. 'Funny thing, that. I suppose it's the first public demonstration they've ever found the courage to make against him. He really seems to be getting under their skins at last . . . '

2

In the weeks that followed, Judie, Tom and Juan knocked about a lot together.

Barrett thought this was a good thing; he liked the two boys and took the view there was less likely to be any serious love-making when Judie was in the company of both than if she had been going around with one only. He did not want to lose her for a few years longer at least.

In many respects Juan and Tom were opposites yet they got on tremendously well together. Juan was the rapier, Tom the bludgeon, big and brawny and almost as fair as Judie. Juan would be apt to act on impulse where Tom would take his time and be very sure of what he wanted before he committed himself. Or so Judie imagined.

She sometimes lay awake for an hour at night wondering how it would feel to be made love to by each in turn.

Juan she thought would be passionate and competent and difficult to keep at bay (provided she wanted to keep him at bay), Tom tender, clumsier and perhaps less insistent. Both, of course, would be completely satisfying.

All this was in the completely unsatisfying realm of imagination. Neither had even attempted to kiss her as yet. Juan, she thought, would be the first to try his luck.

Tom, since his father's departure, had lived in lodgings near the *Verdad* building. Once or twice a week he and Juan would call for Judie and take her to one of the cafes in the Plaza del Castillo, taking it in turns to show her off in the *paseo*. Or she would drive them in the car to explore the neighbourhood of Real Barba and the shores of the Gulf. There were nightclubs and dance halls in the New Town but the atmosphere in them was stifling and they seldom went up there.

Once they hired a rowboat and penetrated a little way into the Everglades. It was a humid twilight world where unseen things moved and made noises, the one place in this scorched land which the sun could not entirely conquer — only on the exposed saw-grass islands did it beat down relentlessly.

After half an hour they came to a stretch where the water-weed made rowing laborious and the foliage met overhead so that the late afternoon sun only penetrated in slanting shafts like the spotlights in some vast green theatre. The men rested on their oars and eyed their passenger in the stern appreciatively.

Tom asked curiously, 'What are you planning to do, Judie — live permanently here in Real Barba or go back to England some time?'

'I don't know,' Judie said thoughtfully. 'I was born here — I suppose it's more my home than England. It depends on a lot of things — '

'Like how much liberty Escobar allows *Verdad*, for instance?' Tom suggested.

She nodded.

'Yes. I don't think Martyn would stay if he felt the paper would never be completely free again. There's always the chance, of course, that General Escobar may turn liberal — or get thrown out.'

'There's always the chance that pigs'll fly. But somehow you don't notice many in the sky.'

'Tom,' Juan broke in, 'your father worked for the oil company once. Did he ever say if he thought Escobar's mob could carry on the wells by themselves?'

'He said they couldn't — not without foreign technicians. He was dead positive about that.'

'Well, then let them bring in foreign technicians,' Juan said shrugging. 'The State of Havamo could still retain ownership and pay the foreigners like ordinary employees. That way Escobar's face would be saved.'

'No,' Tom said. 'The only ones that would come would be Russians. America wouldn't stand for that. She won't interfere herself but she'll make sure nobody else does.'

'Then I think we'll lose Judie,' Juan forecast soberly. 'Without the oil revenues Escobar's got no alternative but grind the people. And in order to persuade them grinding doesn't hurt he must control the press.' He looked at Judie and for a moment the black eyes in the brown face smouldered. 'Personally I'd rather chance letting in the Russians.'

'*Gracias, gracias, amigo mio!*' Judie said lightly.

Tom ran out his oar. Somewhere in the weeds a turtle plopped; a faint miasma was beginning to rise from the rank vegetation.

'It's getting damp — let's go back,' he grunted and began to pull on his oar. Judie imagined a slight edge to his voice, wondered if it could be jealousy and naturally hoped it was.

They turned the boat round and headed back. When they had cleared the Everglades the sun was warm again. As they ran alongside the ramshackle jetty Juan jumped out and tied up the boat.

'I'll tell the *barquero* we're back,' he said and went towards the boathouse.

Tom climbed out and gave his hand to Judie. When she had stepped on to the jetty beside him he didn't release her hand. Instead he pulled her close and held her against him and kissed her hard on the mouth. His body was taut and his hands uninhibitedly possessive and he held the kiss so long she was afraid Juan would have finished with the boatman and would come out and find them locked together.

She pushed him away. He wiped her lipstick from his mouth with the back of his hand and they walked along the jetty without exchanging a word. As they came abreast of the boathouse Juan was standing at the door, a peculiar look on his face.

They all three went up in silence towards the car.

⋆ ⋆ ⋆

The plot of land owned by Pedro Carranza was one of the largest in the isthmus outside the *ganaderias*.

It could not by any stretch of imagination be called fertile but it was one of the least infertile because it lay along the border of the Everglades and occasionally an evening mist would drift across from the swamps and before dissipating bring a suggestion of moisture to its parched surface.

Pedro had a half-breed wife and seven children — four boys and three girls — and the plot kept them all on the right side of starvation.

It measured almost three-and-a-half acres.

Pedro himself was a travelled man, having in his youth worked for a while up in Mexico. He had more intelligence than most of his neighbours, possessed a flair for petty politics and had considerable powers as a demagogue.

In his own eyes he was a yeoman, deriving his freedom from the land which he owned and cultivated. Any sort of restraint, any curtailment of the liberty which he imagined he enjoyed, would have been anathema to him. He expressed his views freely to anyone who cared to listen to them.

Pedro was not a very efficient farmer but it is not impossible that had he lived longer than he did and had the chips fallen right for him he might have become the John Hampden of Havamo.

He was, in fact, the sort of man General Escobar took an interest in.

One forenoon a jeep containing three armed soldiers and a civilian bumped along the track that borders the Everglades. Pedro was standing in a corner of his plot with a two-pronged fork in his hand, looking for something showing above ground that could be dug out and made into a mid-day meal for the Carranza family. He was absorbed by his search but a corner of his mind was also giving attention to the approaching ribbon of dust.

When he saw that the jeep had stopped and three of its passengers had got out and were coming over the dry ridges towards him he stuck his fork into the hard ground and leaned on it and waited for them. He had no fondness for jeeps but did not feel any particular apprehension.

He could see now that the civilian carried papers under his arm and that one of the soldiers was a sergeant and the other a private. He even noticed that the sergeant had a large raised birthmark on his right cheek which he kept touching selfconsciously with his finger as if hoping that some time he would find it had disappeared.

The three men stopped in front of Pedro and the civilian said, 'You are Pedro Carranza?'

Pedro pushed his sombrero a little more over his eyes and nodded affirmation. The official consulted his papers.

'Your tax assessment is thirty-two *quintals of legumbres*,' he said. 'We have come to collect. Where is it stored, please?'

Pedro indicated his three-and-a-half acres with a polite sweep of his arm.

'You are welcome to take whatever you can dig out,' he said. 'Myself, I would be glad to find one little head — just one little green head.'

'Perhaps then you have money set aside in lieu of produce?' the civilian suggested.

Pedro put his head back and laughed with genuine amusement. His wife, hearing the sound, came to the door of their adobe hut and leaned against it and watched.

'*Senor funcionario*,' Pedro said, having quelled his laughter, 'you might, if you search the house carefully, find enough small change to buy three bottles of beer. Mind you, I think it unlikely but it is not utterly impossible. You are welcome to keep whatever money you find.'

The official said stonily, 'I take it, Pedro Carranza, you do not intend to meet this tax assessment?'

Pedro nodded gravely. He was begining to enjoy himself a little.

'You are a man of perception, Senor,' he said.

The official put away his papers and turned to the sergeant.

'The matter is now in your hands, Sergeant Hino,' he said.

Pedro loosened the fork in the ground at his feet but did not withdraw it. The amusement was gradually fading from his eyes. Three or four children had joined their mother in the doorway and were watching the scene with darting alert glances like little monkeys.

The sergeant touched the birthmark on his cheek with his fingers and then snapped them at the private but kept his eyes on Pedro.

'Arrest this man,' he ordered. 'And put handcuffs on him.'

'Please — one moment,' Pedro protested. 'You cannot do it — I have rights — '

'By refusing to pay taxes you've lost any rights you had,' the sergeant snapped. 'This land belongs to the State and someone will be found who can work it profitably. What's more, your family'll be evicted — '

'Get off my land!' Pedro screamed. 'Tell Escobar to . . . ' Here he used an obscene expression accompanied by the universal two-fingered gesture. 'And that goes for the lot of you too, if you can manage it — '

At the same time he wrenched the fork out of the ground and pointed it at the sergeant. 'Come on, you pock-marked bastard!' he added for good measure.

It seems probable he did not intend to

attack the sergeant but merely to frighten him away. In any event the sergeant forestalled him. He whipped out his revolver and fired three times. Pedro dropped his fork, clutched his stomach, swayed on his feet for a moment and then slumped to the ground.

His wife — or rather his widow, for he was already dead — threw herself on the prostrate body. The children in the doorway began to cry.

'You saw, of course, what happened?' the sergeant said to the other two, putting his revolver back in its holster and touching the birthmark with his finger. 'He was going to kill me — I shot in self defence.'

They turned and went towards the jeep. It was quite a small jeep and could not possibly have held thirty-two *quintals*.

As they drove back the sergeant noticed that the dust they had raised in coming had not yet quite settled . . .

* * *

Next day the same tax gatherers paid a visit to the *ganaderia* of Don Luis Ribera.

Don Luis was sitting at the ringside of his small private arena arranging the details of a *tienta* — that is, a testing of bulls and heifers for bravery — which he planned to hold in the coming week.

The sergeant and the civilian came in unannounced and sat down beside him, one on either side. The civilian consulted his papers and mentioned a large sum as being due in respect of tax.

Don Luis had already paid his normal tax which in all conscience he considered ample. He had not at hand — or indeed anywhere in ready cash — a quarter of the additional sum now mentioned.

He explained this frankly, being careful to control his naturally fiery temper. The official then suggested Don Luis should hand over whatever money he had in the house and make up the balance by a delivery of first quality fighting bulls.

The rancher eyed him as he might have eyed a chicken-hearted bull calf and then waved his hand (with a motion very like that of Pedro Carranza the previous day) towards the pastures.

'If you care to collect the bulls and drive them away I can scarcely stop you,' he said.

The civilian looked at Sergeant Hino who remarked curtly, touching his cheek, 'We're not *vaqueros*, Senor. Certainly we could shoot a number of *toros* and have the carcases collected but fighting bulls are of more value alive. I must warn you if you insist on paying your debt in dead carcase meat you'll have very little stock left.'

Don Luis paled. Down in the ring several of his men were leaning against the *barrera*, testing with their fingers the steel tips of their *varas*, which they were selecting for next week. For a moment a crazy idea ran through the breeder's head — then he remembered what he had heard only that morning about Pedro Carranza.

He said with a sigh, 'The English have a proverb about killing the goose that lays the golden egg — but probably you are not literary gentlemen. I've contracted to deliver six bulls to Mexico City in three days' time. I'll let you have the money as soon as they pay me.'

The civilian made a rapid calculation.

'If they are first-class *toros* — '

'One does not send anything else hundreds of miles to the Plaza Mexico,' Don Luis said coldly.

'All right, all right,' the official agreed grudgingly. 'Give me as well what money you have in the house and we'll call it square. You see, we're not unreasonable.'

Don Luis rose wearily. So great had been the effort of self-control he looked and felt as if he had aged ten years in the last few minutes.

The loss of six of his finest bulls would mean a heavy deficit this season and a further grievous lowering of the standard of living of himself and his dependants.

'Come,' he said in a low voice, 'I'll get you the money now.'

Down in the ring one of the *vaqueros*, watching the three men go, remarked to his companion, 'The Senor is failing. I hadn't noticed before how old he's getting . . . '

* * *

Later that day Barrett, sitting alone in his office in the *Verdad* building, got a phone call. General Escobar wanted to see him at four o'clock precisely.

Barrett put the receiver down slowly and sat immobile for long minutes. In spite of his immobility he could feel the perspiration gather at his armpits and trickle down his sides.

He rose and changed his shirt and at five minutes to four got out the car and drove across the Plaza Mayor — feeling, as he always did when he made the short journey, an atmospheric transition from Old Spain to Manhattan.

He had met Escobar face to face only once before, at some function in the early days when the new President still had about him the aura of a possible messiah, the promise of a golden time that would outshine the dull benevolence of Merida. Even Barrett himself, in the glitter and dominance of the new man, had for a while been seduced into forgetting the benevolence of the old order and remembering only its dullness.

He parked his car between the two skyscrapers, on his right the towering Office of Escobar, on his left the palatial residential suites of the President's entourage and camp-followers, male and female.

A square half-mile feeding on fifteen thousand square miles, he reflected — feeding but unsatisfied.

Beyond the steel and concrete giants were the Army barracks and, away in the background, the impotent derricks.

He went through the huge archway on his right, trying to master the uneasiness that gripped him.

The lobby was cluttered with young men in showy uniforms — the new *élite*, he reflected again bitterly, strong-arm thugs, pimps, teddy-boys, the refuse of Havamo masquerading as destiny's white hopes.

He made his business known and was whisked up a dozen storeys and ushered into the presence.

The President of the Republic of Havamo sat behind a huge desk in a magnificently carpeted room. He looked well fed, sleeker than Barrett remembered him, his hair thick and black except where it was greying slightly above the close-set ears, his skin a darker brown than most of his compatriots. The military moustache above the full lips was trim, the heavy jaw sensual, the uniform splendid beyond words — a dapple of red tabs, medals and gold braid.

A glossy man of the world, a man's man and a woman's man, Barrett decided . . . but first of all Escobar's man.

The General did not rise but indicated a chair facing him and pushed forward a box of cigars.

'Well, Senor Barrett,' he said, lighting Barrett's cigar and his own, 'I felt the time was ripe for a chat.'

Barrett nodded but said nothing.

The other went on smoothly, 'So far my demands on your paper's space have been slight. In future I'll need more — say two columns a day in your leader page. Also I thought of issuing directives daily instead of weekly.' The black eyes across the desk settled for a moment on

Barrett's own. 'But first I wanted your reactions.'

The screw turning, Barrett thought, always turning.

He said levelly, 'Two columns a day? It's quite a lot, sir.'

Escobar shrugged.

'Perhaps not every day. It'll depend on circumstances.'

'Well,' Barrett said, thinking fast but trying to keep his voice casual, 'well yes, I suppose it could be done. I take it you'll want me to print the material just as it comes from your office. It might be a good idea to head it 'Supplied by the Office of Escobar', or something like that.'

General Escobar shook his head — but very gently.

'No, Senor Barrett, that would not be a good idea. The whole point is that it must read like an expression of editorial opinion — which I trust it will be. It's the nature of Governments to decline in popularity — I had a reminder of that only the other day at the *corrida*. Editors don't suffer from the same disability, at least not to the same degree. My department will give you the gist of what it wants said, you'll say it in your own words. But the Office of Escobar mustn't on any account be mentioned. Is that clear, Senor Barrett?'

'Quite clear,' Barrett said tonelessly.

General Escobar smiled pleasantly.

'Good,' he said. 'Now let's take a specific example. Up to date the system of taxation has been inefficient, to put it mildly. I'm in process of rectifying that. Naturally the shoe will pinch in places — there'll be unpleasant incidents. It's of the utmost importance such incidents should be presented by the press in a suitable light. You're an intelligent man, Senor Barrett. If you've any questions, please ask them now.'

Barrett took a long pull at his cigar. All right, you bastard, he thought, answer this one.

'I'd like to put forward an even more specific example — Pedro Carranza,' he said, his voice brittle. 'For obvious reasons I didn't report it at all. But two possible methods of presentation did occur to me. He might have been built up as the first martyr of the coming counter rising. Or exposed as an enemy of the people, a murderous fanatic bent on wrecking the legitimate operations of a benevolent government. The latter, I take it, would be a better angle.'

General Escobar did not bat an eye.

'Much, much better — for everybody,' he agreed suavely. 'And also more accurate — for there won't be any counter rising. Since we're being frank I may as well explain one further point which may have puzzled you — my treatment of the oil company. Of course I miss the revenue. But for prestige purposes I considered it necessary to get rid of a foreign company operating on our soil. In time I hope to send some of my young men abroad to learn the techniques so that they can come back and reopen the wells. But that, if it's possible at all, will take years, perhaps many years. In the meantime it'll be official policy not to mention the wells. Let the people forget. And by the way, so long as you and I continue to see eye to eye in these matters you and your paper will be exempt from tax. Well, Senor Barrett, I think that's all for the moment — our little chat was worth while.'

Damn him, he's dismissing me with a bribe, Barrett thought. Maybe the time's come for me to pack the whole thing in and take Judie back to England — I've really got some hard thinking ahead.

He rose to go, grinding out his cigar, but General Escobar had still a final word for him. It was a point of policy of the General's always to make the final salvo the most telling.

'Some day I must take you round the Army barracks,' he said, smiling. 'I've resources there that might surprise you. You have not only yourself to think about now, Senor Barrett — I hear you've given a very pretty hostage to fortune. Oh, and I nearly forgot — from today an exit permit signed by me is required before anyone can leave Havamo.'

He pressed the bell on his desk. As Barrett went down in the lift the perspiration broke out again.

That's it, he thought, he kept it to the end — the very end . . .

* * *

Barrett didn't tell anyone about his interview with Escobar. Neither Judie nor Tom Clark noticed his preoccupation because they were themselves preoccupied — with each other.

This mutual awareness had developed with a speed that shook Judie. One day it wasn't there, the next day it was.

The young people seldom went about as a trio now; somehow it always happened that Juan was left behind.

Tom and she would take the car out and park it at the first opportunity and immediately and with complete naturalness find themselves in each other's arms. Or they would get out at a quiet part of the Gulf shore with the same result.

Tom's love-making was intimate enough but he hadn't as yet attempted the ultimate intimacy. Judie wondered if she would have the will-power to refuse him if he did.

For both of them the world had changed, enlarged, become more exciting, more intense. They were not just a boy and a girl having a good time. They were a man and a woman in love.

Barrett, racking his brains to discover some way of preserving a remnant of freedom for his paper, noticed vaguely that Judie was blossoming and developing with surprising speed and that Tom's occasional fits of moroseness (observable since the British colony's departure from Real Barba) had disappeared. Any woman would immediately have connected the two things but the preoccupied Barrett didn't.

Meanwhile out in the country things were progressing with deceptive slowness. Pedro Carranza's widow had been put off her land and she and her family had bedded down with a neighbouring farmer whose wife had recently deserted him.

Three soldiers were sent to work the Carranza plot and demonstrate that it really could produce the amount estimated in the tax assessment.

It would, of course, be a long time

before the result could be known, but the soldiers had already cheated by secretly saturating the ground with expensive chemical fertilisers which no *peon* could afford.

Barrett, pondering the new directives, believed that Escobar's ultimate objective might be to turn all the plots and *ganaderias* into one vast farm managed by the Department of Agriculture and worked by the former owners who would thus be reduced to something like feudal serfs, living perhaps in communal barracks and allowed to retain only enough of the fruits of their labours to keep them alive, the rest going to the State.

He tried to persuade himself that in actual fact they might not be so much worse off than at present — apart from having to work harder. But in his heart the difference was palpable: they would have lost their freedom and their small stake in the country.

For himself Barrett saw no way of regaining *his* lost freedom. No way, that is, that wouldn't involve Judie in grave peril. He was far removed as yet from an extremity that would compel him to consider that . . .

⋆ ⋆ ⋆

When Juan Ribera heard from his father about the loss of the six bulls he was suddenly filled with a new disgust for despots and despotism.

Maybe his time at the university in California had prepared the way by showing him that there were alternatives. People who had never been outside Havamo — and that meant nearly everyone — lacked even this elementary political sophistication.

Usually when the régime was bad, like the one before Merida, they simply lay low and waited for the next revolution. Once or twice when the thing went on too long the *peons* had stirred themselves — the under-dogs had become wolves — and the current autocrat had been overthrown. But only to make way for the next strong-arm candidate in the queue.

The idea of electing a government for themselves had little part in their political thinking. It seemed unnecessary to go to all that trouble since no government lasted very long anyway.

Until the coming of Escobar.

Perhaps the precise manner of that coming may be briefly interpolated here, though it presented few novel features.

Havamo's oil had been developed by foreign capital and technicians during the latter half of Merida's rule. With his share of the revenues Merida had begun to build up a civil police force, conceiving this a benefit to the people. But within the force a certain Corporal Escobar had a better idea and secretly began to transform the civil organisation into a military one with a shadow chain of command.

When the time was ripe he struck — hard. Merida was assassinated and General Escobar took his place.

For a year thereafter he used the oil revenues to equip his pocket army with the most modern weapons (he would have liked an air force too but the revenues didn't run to that). He paid and fed his soldiers well and kept them contented with such amenities as a steady and varied supply of women.

Then, fearing that the fast-developing oil empire might become as great a power as himself, he got rid of it, hoping that new internal taxation might somehow replace the lost revenues.

This is how it came about that the people of Havamo at last acquired a Government that looked like lasting a very long time indeed . . .

The Riberas, husband, wife and son, were sitting over dinner when Don Luis told about the loss of his six bulls. Juan was silent for a while, his eyes smouldering, then he burst out suddenly, 'Don't you think, father, it's time someone did something to rid us of Escobar?'

'The next revolution will do that,' Don Luis replied tiredly, 'though certainly it's a pity *Verdad* isn't with us. Its attitude may delay matters.'

'The trouble is, will we have any *ganaderia* left by then?' Juan demanded bitterly. 'Already life's hardly worth living.'

Dona Vittoria eyed her son keenly for a moment.

'You sound,' she observed, 'not like a man who has lost six bulls but like one disappointed in love.'

'Oh don't be silly,' Juan exclaimed irritably.

When the meal was over he got up and left the room abruptly. Dona Vittoria looked at her husband, her fine eyes worried.

'Juan's been in a strange mood lately,' she said. 'I hope he's not going to do anything foolish.'

'Like what?' Don Luis enquired absently.

'I don't know. But he's got your recklessness, Luis — the recklessness you had when you were young.'

'Oh the boy's all right,' her husband said, shrugging. 'Naturally he's worried about the finances of the *ganaderia* — after all it'll be his one day. He'll probably go out and ruin one of the *pueblo* girls and then he'll feel better . . . '

⋆ ⋆ ⋆

The offices of a newspaper are seldom entirely deserted. Nearly always someone is within sound of the news-desk phones or servicing the complicated machinery of the presses. Even the editor's hours are long and uncertain. Barrett and Tom spelled each other by mutual agreement; every week they alternated in taking a complete day away from *Verdad*.

On one of Tom's days off he and Judie decided to visit the Christ of Tlazcala. This is perhaps the most famous landmark in Havamo, a gigantic statue built by monks half a century ago on the summit of one of the Cordilleras. The monastery disappeared in the earthquake of 1918 but the statue remains, its outstretched arm pointing towards Real Barba thirty miles away.

There are several small *pueblos* along the road, which peters out on the mountainside. The last three thousand feet have to be climbed on foot.

Maria had made up a picnic lunch which they stowed in the boot of the car. The sun was already on the warm side for comfort; it would be a blazing day. At the first *pueblo* Tom, who was driving, pulled the car up at a cafe that looked reasonably clean.

They got out and sat down on a wooden bench against the adobe wall and a black-eyed Indian girl brought them two glasses of tinned beer. The road was white with dust, the land beyond the colour of burnt sienna. In the distance the blue line of the Cordilleras ran across the horizon like a streak of gouache.

Tom had spoken very little as yet. Now he said, 'Judie, I — I'm not sure how you feel about things,' and stopped.

She sat very still and waited. He took a long drink from his glass and looked away from her along the ribbon of road and said, 'Judie — Judie, will you marry me?'

Quite simply she said, 'Dear Tom — yes, I'll marry you.'

He turned and took her in his arms and kissed her — not urgently as he usually did but gently, almost gratefully. He held her a long time and presently, when she had breath to speak, she said, 'That Indian girl — they'll all see us — '

He grinned happily and said, 'Hell,

what does it matter?' Then he kissed her again, more urgently now, his arms tight about her body. She would have liked it to go on for ever but she heard the girl coming out and pushed him away.

The waitress was standing watching them, a keenly interested smile on her face. Tom, his mouth smeared with lipstick, paid the bill and tipped her enormously. As the car roared away Judie, on a sudden impulse, turned and waved. The girl waved back enthusiastically, shading her eyes with her free hand.

'*Buena suerte!*' she called after them, '*Buena suerte!*' Tom drove fast along the road which soon began to climb. In half an hour it petered out high up on the sierra and they got out, Tom shouldering the knapsack which Maria had packed. Below, the country had begun to assume the appearance of a map, the heat haze giving its hardness a soft beauty as if seen through gauze. Immediately above them to the west a belt of dry forest seamed the otherwise bare mountainside.

It took an hour and a half of hard foot-slogging before they reached the base of the statue.

Hot and breathless they stared up at the towering Christ of Tlazcala, rough hewn but of immense power, its outstretched arm suspended far above.

They sat down in its shadow and opened the knapsack. There was cold chicken and slivers of toasted maize bread, rolled slices of Mexican ham, peaches and pimentos and little pastry cups filled with mixed pickles. At the bottom Maria had slipped in a big bottle of white wine and they shared it equally.

Far below and thirty miles away they could now dimly discern Real Barba and, a little to the left, the airstrip where Judie had landed two months ago. It seemed to her now like a line dividing childhood from womanhood. To the east the blue vastness of the Gulf was just visible through the haze. On either side of them the jagged spine of the Cordilleras stretched away into infinity.

When they had finished they lay back on the swart grass of the mountaintop and rested. Even in the shadow of the Christ of Tlazcala the air was hot and motionless. In the sky above the distant airstrip the sun glinted for a moment on polished metal.

'That'll be Joe Peters,' Tom said lazily.

'Who's he?' she asked.

'Joe's a civil pilot for the Army contractors,' he explained. 'Flies in small arms and stuff like that.'

Presently he leaned over her and took her in his arms again and smothered her with kisses. There was an urgency in his love-making now that stirred in her a willing response. She put her arms round his neck and held him close. The thin material of her blouse was scarcely intended for repelling this sort of assault but she did not care. She wondered, is this it? . . . If it is, I'm glad it's Tom . . .

But he released her and looked down at her and said gently, 'No — no.' Then he grinned irreverently and added, 'Not in the shadow of the Christ of Tlazcala.'

She smiled up at him. 'I'd only have myself to blame, Tom. But please, if you can, keep it till we're married.'

He took one of her hands, not grinning now, and kissed her fingertips gently.

'How long will that be?'

'A little while,' she said. 'We've got to think about it. Marriage is pretty important — there'll be things to arrange first.'

He was thoughtful, then he said anxiously, 'You really did mean it, didn't you? You're not going to change your mind, Judie? I suppose I've got a nerve — setting my cap at the boss's daughter — '

She laughed and pulled down his worried face and covered it with kisses.

'No, Tom — I'm never going to change my mind. You're the one I want.'

All through the rest of the morning and into the long, hot afternoon they talked and talked. And between talks they made love with a gentle, satisfying passion.

Eventually the sun came round the Christ of Tlazcala and slanted down on them and Judie freed herself and looked at her watch.

'Heavens!' she exclaimed. 'It's time we were going.'

She rose and smoothed down her dress and pulled Tom to his feet, and hand in hand they went down the mountain towards the car.

They stopped on the way back at the same *pueblo* and the Indian girl, still smiling and with a question now in her eyes, served them with two more glasses of beer and again Tom tipped her enormously.

On the outskirts of Real Barba a newsboy in a booth was calling a special edition of *Verdad*. Tom pulled in the car for a moment to buy a copy and scan its headlines. Suddenly Judie saw his face go stiff and grim.

'Tom — what is it?' she asked.

He spread the paper over the steering-wheel and she followed the headlines down.

'Oh no,' she whispered. 'No . . . '

The column began: 'This morning an attempt was made on the life of General Escobar by a criminal lunatic who fired three shots at the Liberator as he drove along the Montezuma Highway. By the mercy of providence General Escobar escaped unhurt. The would-be assassin was immediately seized by the incensed crowd and torn to pieces. Papers found on the body show him to have been Juan Ribera, son of the bull-breeder . . . '

* * *

They found Martyn Barrett alone in his office at the top of the *Verdad* building. He was sitting hunched at his desk in his shirtsleeves, an unlit cigar in his mouth.

A copy of the special edition lay open before him. He looked up as Judie and Tom came in and managed a tired smile.

'Well,' he said, 'you kids have a good day?'

They nodded.

'Thank God someone had,' the editor said.

'This story about Juan,' Tom said. 'There's no mistake — ?'

Barrett slowly shook his head.

'No. Father Rafael from the Cathedral happened to be there. He told me about it even before I got the official account. Juan was waiting at the hairpin, knowing the car would slow down there. He fired three times and missed, using an old revolver they kept on the ranch. He wounded the chauffeur slightly, that's all. The damn-fool kid threw his life away for nothing . . . '

Judie said softly, 'He can't have suffered much when the crowd killed him. It would be so quick.'

'It wasn't just like that, Judie,' Barrett said. 'The crowd tried to save him — but Escobar's bodyguard got to him first. They hustled him into the barracks and tortured him for an hour to find out if he had any accomplices. Apparently he hadn't. So then they shot him.'

'That's not what it says in the paper,' Judie said.

Barrett took the cigar out of his mouth; unconsciously he clenched his fist, crushing the cigar to pulp.

'God damn it,' he exploded, 'I print what I'm told to print — you both know that. If one of our reporters hadn't bribed a member of the bodyguard I wouldn't even know how Juan died. Anyway the bare facts are that the kid tried to kill someone and got killed himself instead.

There's a sort of rough justice in that. If the story's true in essentials what does it matter if some of the details get twisted a bit?'

Judie went to the window and stared out. The sun was getting low and long shadows lay across the face of the landscape.

'Where will they bury him?' she asked. 'We could at least put flowers on his grave.'

'They don't want flowers on his grave,' Barrett said harshly. 'Anyway, we'll never know where it is. They'll just dig a hole somewhere secretly at night and throw him in.'

'Poor Juan,' Judie said very softly. 'Poor, poor Juan.' She turned from the window and they saw she had been crying. She came over to her father and kissed him on the cheek. 'And poor Martyn, too.'

There was an unhappy silence. Then Tom asked, 'What about Don Luis — is he all right?'

'Don Luis and his wife are in jail,' Barrett said tonelessly. 'I don't suppose they'll ever get out again. Their *ganaderia*'s going to be taken over by the State and turned into farms — it's been announced already.' He got up like a man almost at the end of his tether and reached for his jacket. 'Well, we'd better all go home. It isn't likely there'll be any more news today.'

Tom glanced at Judie who moved to his side. Their fingers touched and intertwined.

'There's — there's one more item,' Tom said bravely. 'I've asked Judie to marry me, Mr. Barrett. She said she would.'

Barrett paused and stared at him, his jacket half on, his face blank. Then he smiled through his tiredness.

'Well,' he said, 'what d'you know — how stupid can a father get? You young dog — I never noticed it coming on. It's been quite a day, hasn't it?' He held out his hand across the desk to Tom. 'I hope you'll both be very happy — I'm sure you will. And now, Judie, come right back over here and kiss me again . . . '

3

When Joe Peters was flying in supplies for the Army of Havamo he usually loaded up at Ciudad Victoria or Tampico in Mexico.

From either place the flight across the Gulf to Real Barba was over five hundred miles. When the contract had first started Joe used a big freighter with three or four of a crew for some of the stuff was heavy.

Nowadays he used a much smaller plane and mostly flew it solo. The Army was fully equipped long since and all it indented for now was replacement of articles damaged or expended in training, so that Joe's loads consisted in the main of small arms, crates of grenades and suchlike relatively minor items.

In normal weather conditions the trip took him something over three hours. There was no place along the route where Joe could have made an emergency landing with much chance of success, but the contractors' maintenance service was sound and Joe was a good pilot so the need had never arisen.

Joe in the air and Joe on the ground were two very different characters.

He was an American, a big loose-limbed Texan, and when he had delivered his cargo and got it signed for he liked to enjoy himself. Enjoyment for Joe meant drink and women; there was no difficulty about satisfying both these requirements for he earned good money and was certainly not miserly.

Tom Clark had first met Joe more than a year ago.

Tom had been working late and it was nearly midnight when he decided to stretch his legs before turning in. He strolled down as far as the Faena for a nightcap. The place was still full and noisy and Tom, downing his small whisky and soda at the bar inside, noticed that most of the noise seemed to be coming from one corner.

He glanced over and saw a huge young man, obviously an American, sitting at a small table with a girl on either side of him. The man was drunk but by no means incapable.

Tom chanced to be standing in the only spot from which he could have seen what followed. One of the girls caught the American's face between her hands and drew it towards her and kissed him. While he was thus distracted the other girl deftly picked a wallet from his inside pocket and slipped it quickly down the low-cut front of her frock (she was a well-built girl and the extra bulge didn't make much difference).

Tom had long since learnt the virtue of minding his own business but it seemed to him the present case constituted an exception.

He strolled over to the table and, standing behind the girl, put firm hands on her shoulders so that she couldn't rise and said to the American, 'Just check if you've got your wallet, will you?'

The big fellow cocked an eye at him doubtfully. The liquor he had consumed had obviously dulled his wits a bit. He was trying to figure out if this stranger was friend or foe.

Meanwhile the girl was squirming under Tom's grip and Tom himself was getting impatient. From where he stood he had an interesting view of the top corner of the wallet.

'Of course, if you don't care,' Tom said shortly, 'why the hell should I?'

The big man seemed suddenly to decide he was dealing with a buddy. He clapped his hand to his pocket and let rip an unprintable Texan oath.

'I've been robbed!' he roared.

'Take it easy,' Tom advised. 'I know where it is.'

The Texan focused on him a bloodshot eye filled with returning doubt.

'Okay, bud — then let's go get it.'

'We don't need to go far — '

With a quick movement Tom thrust his hand down the girl's frock, grabbed the wallet and handed it over to the American. Around them people were watching with glassy interest.

The girl squirmed out of Tom's grasp, put her tongue out at him and said, 'Gringo pig!' The other girl said, 'Americano bum!' to the big fellow. The two men grinned at each other.

'Well, thanks,' the American said. 'Now that that's sorted out, sit down — what'll you have? I'm Joe Peters.'

The girls seemed to have vanished. Tom sat down.

'A whisky and soda,' he said. 'I'm Tom Clark. I was just thinking of going to bed.'

'I think about it all the time — that's my trouble,' Joe Peters said and made a sign to the waiter. He grinned again. 'Which reminds me, I haven't booked a room. Sort of took it for granted the room would be thrown in.'

'I might be able to put you up,' Tom said. 'My digs aren't very grand but the landlady'll probably be glad of another paying guest for the night.'

The other eyed him seriously now. Obviously the drink was beginning to die on him.

'I'll take you up on that, Tom, if it's not too much of a nuisance — '

'Oh that's all right,' Tom said cheerfully. 'It might have happened to anyone . . . '

Next morning after breakfast as Joe was leaving he gripped Tom's hand so hard that it hurt.

'Lucky for me you were around last night,' he said sheepishly. 'If I can do something for you some time, just let me know. It isn't likely — I'm not an influential person. Still, you never can tell . . . '

* * *

The neighbours of Pedro Carranza, instead of being roused to anger by his death, seemed for a while to become more amenable.

The conviction spread that the soldiers who had been working the Carranza plot would in due season produce the amount of the official assessment. The spirit of competition is the third or fourth strongest urge in human nature, even downtrodden human nature. Perhaps the *peons*, having nothing else left to pride themselves on, began to believe that if the soldiers could do it, so could they.

Since the coming of exit and entrance permits, road blocks had been set up on all routes leading out of the country and a careful watch kept at the ports.

This affected the *peons* not at all for they were not travellers — nor was it primarily aimed at them. Escobar reckoned that if there was a cabal against the régime it would most probably be found in the upper strata of Havamo society. He didn't intend that its members should be able to escape at will beyond the reach of his retribution or, alternatively, attempt to bring in arms and ammunition.

To Martyn Barrett every policy directive from the Office of Escobar was becoming more and more a personal humiliation. Had Judie not been there, he told himself, this was the moment he would have made his bid to break free.

He would have been happy to see Tom and Judie married and safely settled in England, much as he would have missed them. He was pretty sure he had enough influence to get Tom a job on an English paper — a living at least, if not a fat one. But he knew without asking that General Escobar wouldn't let Judie go; her presence in Havamo was too convenient a guarantee that *Verdad* would continue to conform.

Judie for her part increasingly blamed herself for ever coming to Havamo and thereby tightening her father's bonds. Her one consolation was that had she not come she wouldn't have met Tom Clark. But even in that there was frustration. Since it was plainly not a time to offer more hostages to fortune, their marriage seemed to be receding further and further into the future.

Once she and Tom drove out to visit the Ribera ranch. The famous bulls were gone, the pastures were being ploughed up and the house itself remodelled as a barracks to house those who would work the land.

She looked towards the distant Cordilleras and saw the white speck that was the Christ of Tlazcala. It seemed a mockery . . .

⋆ ⋆ ⋆

In certain parts of Havamo a type of *tequila* is unofficially produced which is cheap, potent and apt to bring on a sort of temporary madness. It has been truly said that anyone imbibing *tequila* launches himself on an alcoholic sea to uncharted destinations.

This was the only spirit the majority of the *peons* could now afford.

At one of the smaller *pueblos* outside Real Barba — its population was twenty-seven souls in all — the perversity of Fate one evening brought into conjunction two combustible entities.

One was a party of four *peons*, the other an Army jeep. The former had been drinking liberally all evening; the latter, which contained only one soldier, had broken down within some twenty yards of the wineshop where the men were carousing.

The soldier got out and lifted the bonnet and began searching for the fault. The four *peons* looked on, laughing and jeering good-naturedly at the man's unavailing efforts to restart his vehicle.

At this point everything began to go seriously wrong.

The soldier looked up in disgruntlement and cursed the four men mildly. Three of them cursed him back amicably enough but the fourth laid his finger knowingly to the side of his nose and said drunkenly to his companions, 'This *bastardo* of a soldier has insulted us who are descendants of the Conquistadors. Let us teach him a lesson.'

The four men got up unsteadily from their table and lurched across the dusty road to the jeep. Unfortunately the last speaker took with him his empty *tequila* bottle.

The soldier, tired and perspiring and not wanting to pursue the matter further, grinned and shrugged and said, 'A misunderstanding, *amigos* — '

The four *peons*, crazed by the fumes of the *tequila*, suddenly began to flail wildly at the man, many of their blows falling not on him but on each other.

Even at this stage the soldier would have had little difficulty in escaping had not the ringleader aimed a tremendous blow at him with the stone bottle. By the crowning perversity of this ridiculous affair the heavy missile caught him on the left temple and cracked his skull like an eggshell. He collapsed across the wing of the jeep, blood gushing from his wound.

The four *peons* stood staring at him unsteadily for a while, then staggered back to their homes, babbling incoherently.

Presently their fellow-inhabitants of the *pueblo* came creeping down in the gathering darkness and saw with horror what had happened. Obviously the soldier was dead.

Many of the villagers wept with pity. Not knowing what to do, they did nothing. Next morning they would decide how to deal with the stupid perpetrators of the crime . . .

In the course of the night, however, a searching jeep came quietly along the road and its headlights lit up the tragic scene. Its four occupants got out and examined the immediate surroundings carefully. They went over to the wine shop and found it locked and barred, its proprietor having retired in consternation to his home in the *pueblo*. So they drove quietly back to the Army barracks in the New Town.

Next morning, just before dawn, one of the villagers chanced to look out of his adobe hut and by the light of the failing moon made out a whippet tank with a gun turret drawn up on the road facing him.

In that last moment of his life the tank began to shell the village. Two soldiers with automatic rifles had taken up positions nearby to pick off any survivors who might try to escape. In less than five minutes the eight huts of the village had been reduced to rubble and its twenty-seven inhabitants — twenty-three of whom were entirely innocent — to lifeless and unsightly refuse.

The name of the village was Santa Cruz de Olivenca.

* * *

On the evening of the day following the massacre of Santa Cruz de Olivenca Barrett was visited in his flat by three leading *peons* of neighbouring *pueblos*.

Barrett's flat was on the first floor of a five-storey building. Many of the other flats had at one time been occupied by members of the British colony. Now some were vacant; the tenants of the remainder were from the better-off stratum of Real Barba society. They were almost certainly unsympathetic to Escobar's régime. Nevertheless when his visitors came in Barrett, who was alone at the time, drew the curtains of the room.

The spokesman of the party was one Mateo Avila, whom Barrett knew slightly.

He was a lean dark man about forty and looked to Barrett to be a *mestizo* — that is, of mixed white and Indian parentage. A heavy black moustache divided his face and his eyes were deep-set and unusually piercing. He wore a brightly-coloured *poncho* over one shoulder and carried his sombrero politely in his hand. His speech showed him to be a person of some education — probably he had attended the convent school, Barrett thought.

It also flashed through Barrett's mind that if General Escobar were ever to make out a list of possible trouble-makers, the name of Mateo Avila would doubtless be marked with a cross.

'What can I do for you?' Barrett asked.

'Senor Barrett,' Avila said, bowing, 'we have taken the liberty of calling to ask for your advice.'

Barrett waved them to be seated. They set their sombreros on the floor, fitting each ceremoniously on top of the other. Avila introduced his two companions, naming them Jose Garcia and Nino Perez. Barrett noted that there was about Garcia the look of a fanatic. Nino Perez was younger than the other two, slim and good-looking. Each bowed and murmured '*Senor Caballero*.' Only then did they sit down.

'It is about the affair at Santa Cruz de Olivenca,' Avila said.

Barrett felt a prickle of caution run through the core of his mind. It was by no means impossible that the entry of the three men had been noted and might be reported. Avila's eyes were on him.

'It was a bad business,' Barrett said. 'There seems no doubt who started it.

Unprovoked murder can't go unpunished.'

'Agreed,' Avila said. 'The murderer deserved to be shot. His three companions merited terms of imprisonment — ten years, even twenty. No one could have objected to that.'

One of the other men — Nino Perez — said, 'But that is not what happened, Senor Barrett.' He added softly, 'My brother lived in Santa Cruz, Senor. With his wife and little son.'

Barrett got up and went to the sideboard and poured out four whiskies. He put the four glasses and a box of cigars on a tray and passed it round. When they had helped themselves he said, 'I don't understand why you came to me.' He was perspiring very freely.

Avila drew on his cigar and shrugged.

'You are an editor, Senor Barrett — you get news from all over the world. This sort of thing must have happened before. There must be ways to deal with it. We thought perhaps you might be able to tell us what to do and how to do it.'

'Like what?' Barrett asked.

'Like getting rifles into Havamo,' Avila said. 'We have a few dozen. It would take many thousands.'

'Look,' Barrett said carefully. 'Where would you get arms from? How would you pay for them? And how would you smuggle them in?'

Avila shrugged again.

'America has a vested interest in freedom, Senor Barrett. Also she is generous. She might give them without charge. Escobar cannot watch the whole of both coastlines at once. There must be places where small boats could run in.'

'You can take it from me,' Barrett said briefly, 'America has enough on her plate. Her gun-running days are over. Not only will she not interfere herself, she won't let anyone else interfere — Escobar's no threat to her but the newcomer might be.' He looked round at the three intent faces. 'Anyway, what could a few hundred guerrillas do against a modern, well-equipped pocket army?'

Jose Garcia the fanatic spoke for the first time.

'You underestimate our numbers, Senor,'

he said harshly. 'I could tonight find a thousand men willing to storm the Plaza Mayor Barracks. As you must know it's the headquarters of the Army. It would be worth the risk — '

'It would be mass suicide,' Barrett said quietly. 'There would be no survivors.'

Garcia's eyes gleamed angrily and he half rose to his feet but Avila motioned him to silence.

'I agree with you, Senor Barrett,' he said. 'What alternative do you suggest?'

'So long as the Army remains loyal to Escobar there is nothing you can do.'

Avila scowled.

'In my own thoughts that's where I always arrive. I had hoped, Senor Barrett, you would be able to see further along the road than I.'

Barrett's mind was thinking of many things. But most of all he was thinking of Judie.

He said lamely, 'I have nothing to suggest.'

He was conscious that the atmosphere in the room was subtly changing, becoming less friendly.

He blundered on, 'There's a famous character in English literature called Mr. Micawber — he was always waiting for something to turn up. Sometimes it's wiser to — well, just to wait for something to turn up.'

Avila said, brushing this nonsense aside, his thin lips curling, 'Your paper is called *Verdad* — Truth. Once it was well named, but not now. It made the massacre read like a playful scuffle. You've lost your own freedom, Senor Barrett. For that reason, we argued, this man — this fellow-sufferer — will do his best to help us.'

Barrett flushed. He felt humiliated suddenly to a degree he had never before experienced.

He said unsteadily, 'I — I have a daughter — '

He broke off. The eyes of the three men were on him. The *peons* of Havamo have a tremendous sense of family. Some of the friendliness was coming back into their faces. Barrett braced himself to say the thing he had never yet expressed to another human being.

He said in a low voice, 'Escobar warned me that if I get out of line my daughter will be punished as well as myself. I — I love her very dearly. I suppose, to use the old heroic *cliché*, I should love truth and freedom and honour more. Unfortunately I haven't that sort of courage.'

There was silence. The three *peons* sat quietly, uncomfortably, on the edge of their chairs, turning their glasses in their hands. Even Garcia's face had softened.

Then Avila said, 'But you are with us, Senor Barrett?'

'In spirit,' Barrett told him, 'yes, I'm with you.'

He knew it must sound fatuous and insincere. These men could now feel towards him nothing but contempt. He wondered if they would even accept his sworn word to keep this abortive interview secret.

And then he looked into their faces again and realised no such assurances would be necessary or asked for — these people still trusted him as he trusted them.

Avila quoted a Havamo proverb,

smiling faintly but with understanding and not mockingly.

' 'He who hath a daughter has wings on his shoulders to lift him up but weights on his feet to keep him down'.' He seemed to be searching about for something to salvage from the wreck of the visit. 'Some day circumstances may alter — and then you would, perhaps, be with us in more than spirit, Senor Barrett?'

'Some day, perhaps,' Barrett said. 'I make no promises.'

'But if you had advice to give us, you would send us word?' The voice was gently insistent.

'Yes — I'd try to send you word.'

Avila finished his whisky and set down his glass; his two companions did the same.

'Then we must have patience — we must be like your Senor Makkibor and wait for something to turn up.' His eyes rested for a moment on Jose Garcia. 'Perhaps you have at least convinced those of us who would be rash of the folly of rashness. For the moment we must be content with that.'

The three *peons* rose and picked up their sombreros. The sterile interview was over. One by one they shook hands with Barrett and said, 'Good-bye, *amigo*.'

When they had gone he stood irresolutely in the middle of the room for long minutes. Nothing had happened and everything had happened. He had declared himself.

He went over to the sideboard and poured himself another stiff whisky.

⋆ ⋆ ⋆

The position of the churches in Havamo was no better than that of the *peons* or of *Verdad*.

In the cathedral Father Rafael had preached a sermon condemning the massacre of Santa Cruz de Olivenca. On the following day he was summoned to appear before General Escobar.

The little priest made the journey barefoot and declined to sit when invited to do so by the General.

'As you wish,' Escobar said coldly. 'I

shall not keep you long. I merely want to warn you that if you criticise the régime again your church will be closed and you yourself will be exiled. Should you attempt to return you'll be imprisoned. Provided you make no further reference, veiled or otherwise, to matters which do not concern you, you will not be interfered with. Please make this known to your colleagues for it will apply equally to every priest in Havamo. Is that quite clear?'

'There are no matters which are not a legitimate concern of the Church,' Father Rafael said stoutly. 'The Church will still be here long after you have gone.'

General Escobar eyed him impassively; his fingers began to tap very gently on the desk.

'I'm not going to bandy theological arguments with you,' he said evenly. 'But this I would say and would ask you to believe — if necessary I can persecute as ruthlessly as a Hitler. Will you obey, Father Rafael? Think well before you answer.'

The little priest, standing there in his

bare feet, pondered long and carefully, trying to project his mind far into the future, perhaps even as far as two or three decades from now.

'If I obey,' he said, 'it will not be because I fear you or what you can do to me. It will be because I consider — and God grant I'm not presumptuous — that a Church gagged for a little while is better than no Church at all.'

'Your reasons don't interest me in the slightest,' Escobar said. 'You haven't answered my question.'

'I will obey,' Father Rafael said in a voice so low that the man at the desk could only just catch the words. Then the priest crossed himself and raised his eyes. 'Father forgive them for they know not what they do.'

He turned on his bare heel and walked towards the door. As he reached it, General Escobar spoke again.

'You make a mistake, Father Rafael — I know very well what I do. Remember, you have given your word . . . '

4

True to tradition the under-dogs had whelped another wolf.

Following the abortive meeting in Barrett's flat, Garcia the fanatic had finally decided to diverge from the moderates. His boast had been no idle one; he had an underground following of nearly a thousand young extremists, all pledged to the overthrow of Escobar.

Unhappily only about a score of them were armed; it was in the hope of getting more rifles that Garcia had joined the delegation to Barrett.

When that had failed Garcia decided to revert to his original plan, the essential preliminary step of which had been taken long ago.

Jose Garcia was a married man, a *peon* farmer in his middle forties with one grown-up son, Ramon. Three years earlier Ramon, at his father's suggestion, had enlisted in Escobar's Army.

He proved himself a model soldier, soon built up a reputation for dependability and eventually rose to be sergeant-assistant to the Captain in charge of Armoury. When the Captain was off duty the keys of the Armoury passed to Sergeant Ramon Garcia. This had been a greater stroke of luck than either father or son had dared hope for.

Now, a week after the meeting in Barrett's flat, a prearranged message meaningless to outsiders was passed by word of mouth round the thousand members of the cabal . . .

Oddly enough on the same day a company of Pioneers from the Plaza Mayor Barracks began to dig an immense rectangular pit in the suburbs of Real Barba. Passers-by surmised that the foundations of some new military building were being laid . . .

* * *

In the afternoon hour following siesta the immense Plaza Mayor is normally thronged with people. On most days if an additional thousand were thrown in they would not noticeably increase the congestion.

On this particular day the great square looked no different from other days. The sun beat down relentlessly, burning out all colour and reducing the picture to black and white.

At the open gates of the barracks the routine two sentries paced to and fro, to and fro, rifles on shoulders.

In time of peace soldiers do not habitually carry their rifles about with them. Rifles are issued for specific occasions such as parades or exercises; it is only the guards at a few focal points who live with their arms.

In spite of the heat some score of men in the crowd carried *ponchos* folded across their shoulders. A *poncho* is an oblong piece of cloth with a slit in the middle for the owner's head. The *peons* use it for many purposes — as cape, groundsheet, over-blanket, cushion.

The sentries did not notice that these score were gravitating, apparently quite aimlessly, towards the gates.

Suddenly the two nearest the gates whipped rifles from the folds of their *ponchos*. Before the sentries could bring their own weapons from their shoulders two shots rang out. The sentries fell to the ground and lay motionless.

In the Plaza Mayor the introduction of the death-theme made an instant cleavage. The uncommitted majority surged away from the gates, anxious only to escape embroilment. The committed thousand surged towards and through the gates, those few with rifles leading the attack.

The guard-room adjoining the gates was immediately overrun, the Guard Commander and the two relief guards killed. In a matter of minutes the thousand revolutionaries, flushed with this easy initial success, were inside the deserted barrack square.

On the left side of the square stood the Armoury, forming part of the main building; a little beyond it was the big doorway — closed at the moment — leading to the soldiers' billets.

This was the quarter from which the

counter attack was expected. The few men with rifles lined up in front of it, their weapons sighted on the doorway.

Meantime Jose Garcia had made straight for the Armoury, the main body of his followers forming a rough queue behind him ready to pass the rifles back from hand to hand.

Inside the Armoury the waiting Ramon Garcia unlocked the steel door and threw it open. Father and son grinned at each other briefly then hurried to the racks on which stood row upon row of gleaming rifles.

In ten minutes some thousand rifles had been handed out. In the open square a thousand faces lit up with a new certainty of victory as a thousand pairs of hands hefted and fondled the well-cared-for weapons.

Ten minutes. And still no sign of a counter attack . . .

Inside the Armoury Jose Garcia laughed exultantly.

'Their courage has gone with their rifles,' he said to his son. 'By the time they send for help it'll be too late. And Avila thought we couldn't do it!' He clapped his son on the back. 'Now for the ammunition — hurry, *muchacho*, hurry — !'

Ramon swung round to the opposite wall and unlocked the ammunition strong-room. He threw back the heavy doors with a clang — and stood aghast.

The strong-room was empty.

The Barracks Commandant turned away from a window high in the wall above the barrack square. He had deliberately waited until the rifles were handed out; the higher hopes are raised the more painful it is when they are dashed.

'Now!' he said crisply.

In the room behind him a lieutenant pressed a button. The great metal gates below swung together and locked automatically, sealing the square. The body of one of the sentries got in the way but the heavy gate threw it aside.

The Commandant took a revolver from its holster and discharged a shot through the open window into the air.

At the signal an aperture opened in each of the four turrets above the corners of the square and the muzzles of machine-guns ran out through metal shields.

Moving into position the guns made a slight noise and the men below, already startled by the shot from the window, heard this new noise and turned and stared up at the turrets in unbelief. On their foreheads a cold sweat of terror broke.

Inside the Armoury, which might at a pinch have sheltered fifty men, a similar aperture opened high in the wall and a muzzle crept forward.

For a space complete silence reigned in the great square.

Then Jose walked slowly out of the Armoury and looked about him, very pale now, the planning of three years a tragic ruin. He made a pathetic little gesture of apology to his followers. In a sudden burst of impotent rage he shook his fist in the air as if at Fate and discharged his rifle at one of the turrets.

The bullet whined derisively as it impinged on the metal shield and ricochetted harmlessly into the brazen sky.

Those few of his men who had rounds left in their rifles followed his example. Some had two rounds, most had only one. In one of the turrets somebody laughed.

Jose Garcia turned towards the sound and threw out his arms in appeal.

'Kill me,' he shouted, 'but let these men go! It was my idea — all mine — I talked them into it. For pity's sake let them go — !'

In answer a short burst of fire ripped out from the turret. Garcia the fanatic coughed, blood spurted from his mouth and he crumpled up in a series of jerks like a puppet collapsing.

Panic seized his followers. It is difficult to be brave when not even the dignity of a token resistance remains.

They threw themselves on the great iron gates and shook them, whimpering like trapped animals. They clawed at the smooth walls of the square until their scrabbling nails were torn off. They began to run from point to point of their prison, hurling themselves blindly against solid masonry.

A few sought safety in the Armoury, saw the muzzle in the wall and ran out again.

And then the machine-guns began to fire at leisure.

Methodically the thousand men were cut down in swathes as a reaper cuts corn. Some died instantly, some writhed in agony before the life left them, some few escaped miraculously for a matter of minutes, running like frightened hens in zig-zag bursts through the hot square.

The machine-gunners made a game of it with these survivors, taking it in turns to test their marksmanship, touching the trigger so lightly that only two or three bullets spurted out at a time.

But at last — whether by accident or design it is impossible to say — only Sergeant Ramon Garcia remained alive. He had fled from the charnel house of the Armoury and now in the last stages of terror and exhaustion was jinking about the square, leaping over the corpses with which it was littered. His executioners with fiendish skill spattered bullets about his heels as he ran but forbore for a while to finish him off.

Then in the last moments of his life he found his lost courage and stood still and threw back his head and laughed and made rude gestures of defiance at the turrets.

So his tormentors, tired of their sport, pumped a final burst of lead into him and he died still gesturing obscenely.

For some minutes the hush of death again lay over the Plaza Mayor Barracks.

Then gates and doors were opened and fifty lorries drove into the square. Escobar's soldiers came out from the barracks and loaded the vehicles with the thousand corpses.

There was no haste, no improvisation; the thing might have been a routine fatigue.

When the lorries had been filled they were driven through silent streets to the rectangular grave which had been dug in the suburbs. Beside the grave the Pioneers were waiting patiently, spades in hands . . .

Back in the barrack square the rifles were collected and returned to the

Armoury. Then more soldiers appeared with hoses and washed down the crimson square and presently all visible traces of Garcia's rising had been removed.

In the room upstairs the Commandant lifted a receiver and rang through to the Office of Escobar. He waited a moment and then he spoke.

'Sir,' he said, 'H.Q. Commandant reports successful completion of Operation Rat-trap. Yes, sir, exactly as planned — casualties were limited to the five guards who, as arranged, had been kept in ignorance . . .'

⋆ ⋆ ⋆

Garcia the fanatic had made one mistake. He had overlooked the possibility that the cabal, like the Armoury, might contain a spy.

⋆ ⋆ ⋆

The full magnitude of the disaster took a long time to percolate through to the mass of the people. The Office of Escobar made no mention of it, knowing that silence would increase the horror.

An armed guard was placed over the mass grave. Wives awaited husbands, parents awaited sons. Only when absence became prolonged was the dreadful certainty admitted.

The conviction grew that the régime was invulnerable.

Even Mateo Avila began to wonder if there could be any sort of resistance that was not a futility.

5

Since Garcia's defeat Barrett had begun to drink a little more than his usual allowance. On his way home at nights he would drop in at the Faena and down four or five quick whiskies.

Then one night he found what he was looking for. Joe Peters was back in town, sitting at a table in a corner on his own, idly pulling at a cigarette. Barrett had known him a long time; they waved a greeting at each other and Barrett took his drink over to the Texan's table.

'Mind if I join you, Joe?' he asked.

'Help yourself,' the pilot said with a friendly grin. 'How's the press lord?'

'Envious,' Barrett told him. 'Envious of anyone able to soar into the sky and breathe the clean air up there.'

Peters gave him a searching glance.

'Reckon I won't be breathing this particular air much longer,' he said. 'The contract's running out. Another trip should about wrap it up.'

Barrett finished his drink thoughtfully.

'What'll you have, Joe?'

'Let's stick to whisky — last time I mixed them a lady frisked me.'

Barrett ordered two whiskies.

'Won't they renew the contract?' he asked.

'Nope, they don't need to. This time I brought in a few thousand rounds to replace those expended on Garcia's poor devils. Apart from that the Army's well stocked up — they won't need anything big for a long time. When they do they can send in a separate order. It'll be cheaper that way — I guess cheapness is becoming increasingly important to Escobar.' He ground out his cigarette. 'Can't say I'll be sorry to quit. As a customer the General's beginning to stink.'

'So your entrance-exit permit'll be expiring,' Barrett remarked.

The pilot gave him another keen look.

'Yep.'

The waiter brought their drinks, set them down and went away again. Peters glanced round the nearest tables; there was no one within hearing.

He asked quietly, 'Just how badly do you want out, Martyn?'

Barrett lit a cigar. He offered Peters one but the American shook his head and started another cigarette.

'I don't,' Barrett said. They were both speaking in undertones now. 'But I could use a permit for my daughter.'

'Not a chance — not even of getting a forged one. But it might be possible — mind you I say might — to fly out a stowaway. It would need a hell of a lot of considering.'

'Would five hundred pounds help you consider, Joe?'

'Sure would,' Peters said, grinning. 'Come to think of it those airstrip guards sort of take me for granted, I've been coming so long.'

'There'd be two people,' Barrett said. 'Not just my daughter.'

'Now hold on!' Peters protested. 'Two wouldn't make it just twice as difficult — they'd make it all of ten times worse.' He gulped down his drink and signed to the waiter to bring two more.

'All right,' Barrett said. 'A thousand.'

'Who's the other stowaway — yourself?'

The waiter brought the drinks and they talked about something else until he went away again. Then Barrett said, 'No — my daughter's fiancé. Fellow called Tom Clark.'

Peters halted his glass half-way to his mouth and set it down.

'Tom Clark — not Tom Clark?' he said. 'Hey, that's different.'

'How different?' Barrett asked, puzzled.

'About a thousand pounds different,' Peters said, grinning. 'I'll take them both for nothing.'

Barrett took a long pull at his cigar and eyed the Texan doubtfully, wondering how long he'd been sitting there drinking.

'I don't get it, Joe,' he said. 'This isn't the sort of thing I want to kid about — '

'Me neither. Tom Clark did me a favour once. This would sort of square it.'

'It's a pretty expensive pay back.'

'Tom's a pretty nice guy,' Peters said briefly. 'When would they be coming?'

'Don't know yet — I'd have to talk

them into it first, which won't be easy,' Barrett admitted. 'I don't suppose it matters much where you put them down, just so long as it's over the border. There's one thing more. If and when it comes off, I want you to tell them there's only room for two stowaways on the plane. Not three — you understand, Joe?'

The American downed his drink in one long slow gulp and put the glass down thoughtfully.

'Nope, can't say I do — except I suspect you're trying to do the right thing by Tom and his girl, as a good daddy should. Well, if that's the way you want it — '

'That's the way I want it, Joe.'

'Okay,' Peters said, 'let's see, then. I'll be back in a fortnight — we'll have to do it then if we do it at all because it'll almost certainly be my last trip. I'll try to have something worked out. Oh and I'll do my damnedest to keep the three of us out of jail or worse but I'm making no promises. Okay?'

'Okay and thanks, Joe,' Barrett said. 'Of course I mayn't be able to talk them into it. In which case I wouldn't need you after all.'

Peters grinned.

'That'd be okay, too,' he said. 'Oh boy, that really would be okay . . . '

* * *

Although Tom and Judie wanted to get married more than anything else on earth, their impatience didn't blind them to the fact that Havamo in the days of Escobar was scarcely the sort of place where prudent parents could contemplate rearing a family.

Neither could they conceal from themselves that their lovemaking was becoming a frustration rather than a joy.

Barrett timed his introduction of the escape theme with some care. Tom usually dropped in to see Judie in the late evening, or they would come in together, and Barrett would leave them alone in the room overlooking the Everglades.

On a night when a full moon hung in the hot sky like a lantern seen through gauze he left them to themselves a little longer than usual and coughed at the door before he went in carrying a tray on which were two generous whiskies and a sherry. Judie and Tom were sitting at either end of the couch.

'Thought you two kids might like a drink,' he said casually.

'Certainly would, Mr. Barrett,' Tom murmured with unusual formality.

'For God's sake,' Barrett grinned, 'my baggage of a daughter calls me Martyn, it's high time you did too. You're practically my son-in-law.'

Judie curled up her shapely legs under her. 'Practically my foot,' she groaned. 'In another ten years we'll probably still be engaged.'

Barrett served them with their drinks, took his own and sat down in an armchair facing them. He lit a cigar, noting through the flare of the match that the young people were a little flushed. At least they're in the right mood, he thought.

'Judie was just saying if only the three of us could get out of Havamo it would solve everything,' Tom remarked. Barrett, amused, noted he was making conversation with the laboured unease of one addressing a parent to whose daughter one has just been making love. 'But even if we could I said you mightn't like to abandon the paper, Mr. Barrett — Martyn.'

Barrett blew out a cloud of cigar smoke and watched it ascend.

'Oh I'd leave *Verdad* like a shot, Tom,' he said. 'It would be better dead than the sham it is.' He grinned at them. 'But why the three of us? I'm not planning to marry anyone.'

Judie cocked an eye at him. 'What are you up to, Martyn?' she asked quietly.

He looked at her with injured frankness.

'Not up to anything, honey. Maybe the best thing's just to go on as we are — but again, maybe not. Like yourselves I've been thinking about things a good deal lately. The alternative I had in mind involves a certain degree of risk for you and Tom.'

'And for you?' she asked suspiciously.

He shook his head.

'That's why I feel a bit ashamed suggesting it. There's no risk for me, I'm not involved.'

'Go on, please,' Judie said.

'Well, a few nights ago I ran into Joe Peters, the chap who flies in the stuff for the Army. In the course of conversation he mentioned that the airstrip guards aren't very strict with him. He thought he might be able to get a couple of stowaways out of Havamo.'

'But why only a couple?' she asked. 'Why not three?'

'It's a small plane, wouldn't hold more than two besides the pilot.'

Tom said, 'It's a Dragon with extra tanks fitted so that it won't need to refuel between here and Mexico. Even so it should be able to crush in four.'

Barrett shrugged.

'Joe said not. He should know. Maybe he has to take back worn-out bits of equipment or something.'

'I don't see how he's to smuggle us aboard without the guards knowing,' Judie put in. 'Even if he did, Escobar would soon hear that Tom and I were missing. Then he'd put you in jail or worse. And when Joe Peters came back he'd be arrested too.'

'Joe wouldn't be coming back, the contract's finished,' Barrett said. 'As for me, I'd simply deny all knowledge, say you eloped without telling me. Escobar's no fool. So long as I continue to be useful to him by printing his stuff he won't touch me.'

Judie and Tom were silent for a bit, thinking this over and sipping their drinks. Barrett said nothing, giving them time to get used to the idea.

Presently Judie said very earnestly, 'You'd have to promise you wouldn't fall out with Escobar. I've only just found you, Martyn. It would be bad enough losing you again for a while. I don't want to lose you for ever.'

There had been a little catch in her voice; Barrett said quickly, 'I give you my word — '

'Just a minute,' she interrupted. 'Once I told you that when the right time came I'd want you to stand up to Escobar. I've changed my mind. One man can't fight

Escobar nor can a thousand — I know that now. The only thing that's important is that nothing should happen between the time we left and the time you joined us again. If you did anything to anger Escobar he'd kill you, Martyn, just as ruthlessly as he killed Garcia's men and the people of Santa Cruz.'

She was watching his face closely.

'Look, honey,' he said, 'I don't want to lose you either and I don't intend to. Whatever Escobar tells me to print, I'll print. I know when I'm licked. You must accept that.'

He had done it without actually lying. They sat looking into each other's eyes. Then Judie said softly, 'I don't think you'd tell me a whopper — not about anything so important.'

Tom had been silent but now he chipped in. Oh hell, Barrett thought, why can't he leave well alone?

'This thing about you joining us later — I can't see how you'll manage it,' Tom said. 'If Joe's not coming back and if you can't get an exit permit, what other way is there?'

'Well,' Barrett said, 'I haven't worked it out fully but there are several possibilities. For one thing, Escobar's need of propaganda will certainly diminish as he gets things organised his way. My usefulness to him will become correspondingly less. Before very long he'll probably be damn glad to get rid of me. And for another, although Joe's the contract pilot and the contract's running out, there'll always be the occasional order and somebody'll have to fly it in. I'll see if Joe can fix anything there.'

'Sounds a bit dicey to me,' Tom said.

Barrett felt it sounded a bit dicey himself. He had to get Tom off this tack.

'What really worries me,' he said, grinning, 'is will you two remember to get married before you start having babies?'

'We'll remember all right,' Tom said, grinning back at him. 'Matter of fact, before you came in we'd been planning what we'd do if we ever did get out. I thought the best thing would be to get in touch with my dad. He'd probably be good for a job.'

'That's a good idea,' Barrett said,

steering the conversation. 'But there'd still be plenty of problems. Like finding a house, for instance.'

'We thought of that too,' Judie said. She finished her drink and set the glass down and her voice took on a sort of wistful eagerness. 'What we'd like is a small house in a suburb, with a tiny garden. Near enough to Tom's business so it wouldn't be too expensive travelling in and out. We may have to take a flat for a bit while we look around, but most flats don't have gardens and the children would miss that. Before they come I could get a job too, of course — '

'Hold on a minute,' Barrett prompted, 'you haven't got the furniture in yet — unless you're thinking of a furnished place.'

Judie shook her head definitely.

'No,' she said, 'we don't want a furnished place. They put old bits of stick in that look all right at first but soon you find they're breaking up. We might have to do it on the instalment plan, but that's all right so long as you do it sensibly. We could start with the important things first — a table and a few chairs and a — a bed. We wouldn't try to do everything at once. I think that's where so many people get off to a bad start.'

'You really have given it a lot of thought, haven't you?' Barrett said. He wondered where all this was going to take place — Mexico, America, Canada?

They went on like this for nearly half an hour, Judie and Tom doing most of the talking and Barrett putting in an odd word to keep it going in the right direction.

In the end he thought it wise to veer back a bit in case they had forgotten about the link that was to carry them from their present uncertainties to this idyllic future.

'You'd better not build too much on this,' he said. 'Remember, we're not even sure Joe'll be able to get you out. Even if he can, we may consider his plans too risky. I just don't want you to be too disappointed if we have to call the whole thing off.'

But Judie hadn't forgotten. 'Martyn, darling, that wouldn't be the worst thing,' she said softly. 'The awful bit will be when we're saying good-bye and not knowing when we'll see you again . . . '

They went on doggedly discussing the project until the moon had disappeared from the big window. It was the most difficult piece of advocacy Barrett had ever tried to swing but when, exhausted, he finally got to bed he was satisfied he had succeeded.

6

It was getting dark when Joe Peters drove out from Real Barba to the rather primitive airfield for his last return flight to Ciudad Victoria.

He paid off his taxi on the Montezuma Highway and strolled whistling and with his hands in his pockets on to the aerodrome. The Dragon was where he had left it, on the big square of tarmac near the refuelling shed.

Away to the left he could see the dark, clumped line of trees which fringed the east side of the 'drome — the side that had only concrete posts and wires to keep out cattle. On his right were the administrative offices, the customs and guard rooms, the sparsely-furnished passenger lounges. These were all low buildings; behind and above them rose the forty-foot-high control tower.

The latter, he knew, contained a

searchlight though he had never seen it turned on.

The blue lights on the runway were already lit. Everything seemed normal.

An armed guard, hearing his footsteps, looked out of the Customs shed in the half light. Joe passed his hand across his face from left to right in greeting and the guard lifted his own hand in reply and said, 'Okay, Joe.' The man turned and went back into the shed and Peters followed him in.

When charter or big line planes — rare now — were coming or going, or with strangers, the guards were alert enough but everyone knew the Army contractors' pilot. Most of them had had a drink with him at some time or other.

Joe thought, better not tell them it's my last trip, just stick to the old routine.

He went across to the Permits Inspector and fumbled for his permit and the other papers but the man waved them aside. 'We know you got 'em, Joe,' he said. 'Anything to declare?'

It was an old joke between them because this man had nothing to do with luggage examination. Joe said, 'Yeah, I declare to God I wish I hadn't to leave your fair city tonight. There's a new *gallina* at the Faena.'

'What's she like, Joe?'

Joe made wavy up-and-down lines with his hands.

'Like that and everything in its place.'

'Maybe I'll break her in for you, Joe,' the man grinned.

'I've a suspicion she's fully trained,' Joe said and moved on through the swing-doors to the Customs counters.

There were three officials lounging about but none of them showed any particular interest in him. One of them had two red stripes on the cuff of his uniform.

Joe suddenly remembered the two holdalls he had left in the plane earlier that afternoon when the Customs shed was closed. One was Judie's and the other Tom's — Joe had stipulated that one small case each was his limit. He had his stories ready in case of need. Tom's bag didn't need any explaining, a pilot being entitled to a little hand luggage. Judie's ostensibly belonged to one of Joe's numerous girl friends who was sending a few part-worn clothes to her married sister in Mexico.

To be on the safe side Joe saluted the man with the two stripes.

'There's a couple of bags in the Dragon, Pepe,' he said. 'Want to have a look?'

'Just bags, Joe?' Pepe asked.

'There might possibly be a bottle around somewhere,' Joe said. 'But only a small one — honest.'

'Okay,' Pepe said. 'You going now, Joe? I'll get someone to ring the tower — '

'Hold it a bit, Pepe,' Joe said. 'The port engine coughed once or twice coming in. Think I'll taxi her round first and see if she's got rid of it.'

'You're supposed to get a mechanic to check,' Pepe demurred but without interest. 'Mebbe I can get you one — '

'Shouldn't imagine that's necessary,' Joe told him casually. 'I'll let you know if it's serious.'

He went out to the tarmac and climbed into the Dragon and started up the engines, the starboard first and then the port. The port really had missed a couple of times coming in and he was delighted when it did it again now — Pepe could hardly help but hear.

He taxied her out and turned her along the approach strip towards the trees.

Suddenly the searchlight went on in the control tower and swivelled about before coming to rest on the perspex dome of the Dragon's cockpit. Joe breathed an obscene oath and leaned forward to let the man see who he was and pointed towards the port engine. But the radio crackled and the searchlight still stayed on so he picked up the earphones and held one to his ear.

'That you, Joe?' a voice said. 'What the hell you think you're doing? You haven't been cleared.'

'As if I didn't know,' Joe grunted into the mike. 'Who's that — Pablo or Nieto?'

'Pablo.'

'Well listen, Pablo,' Joe said and explained about the engine.

'I'll keep the light on you,' Pablo offered.

'Thanks but don't bother — I know this field like I know the palm of my hand. Nothing coming in, is there?'

'No, but — '

'Then what can I hit?' Joe said. 'Blow out your candle and go back to sleep, *hombre*.'

'Bloody American,' Pablo said amicably.

But the searchlight went out. Joe put down the earphones with a puff of relief and revved the engines slightly and taxied on towards the trees.

He was dead tail-on to the control tower now but when he neared the boundary he brought her round at right angles so that the door was on the side furthest from the tower.

He calculated he was about a quarter of a mile from the tower. It was getting really dark now.

When he came precisely opposite the seventh tree in the clump he stopped the plane and, moving as fast as a big man could in the confined space, opened the door and ran out the ladder. Almost before it was down two figures darted out from the shadow of the trees and, keeping the plane between themselves and the tower, clambered into the cabin. He noted with approval that the smaller figure was in jeans.

Joe left Tom to pull up the ladder and shut the door and by the time the searchlight came on again he was back in his seat at the controls. He knew without looking that Tom and Judie would by now be tucked well down the tail and out of sight.

He calculated the door had been open for thirty seconds which was exactly what they had counted on. He knew also that Pablo would be looking at him through binoculars down the line of the beam so he made the thumbs-up sign and revved the engines and pretended to be listening to the sound of the blades.

Both screws were turning sweetly now. The light went off again and Joe turned the Dragon and taxied leisurely back towards the apron.

'There's a mattress back there,' he said over his shoulder. 'Get down on it both of you and don't make a cheep till I give the all clear.' He added, grinning to himself, 'And for Pete's sake don't forget you're not married yet — this 'ere's a respectable old plane.'

He heard Judie chuckle and decided she must be a pretty brave girl even to pretend to be amused with Escobar's minions metaphorically breathing down her neck.

When he got to the start of the runway he left the engine turning over, climbed out and strolled nonchalantly back to the Customs shed. He was careful to leave the door of the plane open as if he had nothing to hide.

'How was it, Joe?' Pepe asked.

'She's okay, Pepe,' he said. 'Sweet as a nut. I'll be pushing along now.'

Pepe nodded to one of his underlings.

'Ring the tower and tell them Joe's cleared and ready to go,' he said. Then he came over to Joe and put a hand on his shoulder. 'Now let's take a look at that bottle of yours, *amigo mio*,' he added.

Joe suddenly felt as if he had been clubbed. He hoped it didn't show in his face. He had forgotten that Pepe regarded the amiable confiscation of bottles as one of his perks.

'Sure,' he said evenly. 'But make it snappy, Pepe. I gotta get off — I'm late as it is.'

They walked back towards the plane, Pepe's hand still on his shoulder. The man was talking, almost certainly meaning to be friendly, but Joe didn't hear a word of what he was saying.

When they came to the open door he thanked his stars he hadn't let the ladder down again. It required a considerable physical effort to climb in without it but for a tall man like himself it wasn't really difficult. A small man would need to be pretty fit to do it at all. Pepe was about five feet six and fat.

Joe said, 'I'll get you that bottle,' and hoisted himself quickly into the Dragon. He was just about to slam the door in Pepe's face and take his chance of getting her off the ground before the bullets began to fly when mercifully the radio crackled.

He picked up the earphones.

'Plane signalled from Tuxicala,' Pablo's

voice said urgently. 'If you're not up inside a minute you'll have to wait, Joe.'

He turned quickly to Pepe; by the mercy of providence the man hadn't stuck his head in through the door.

'Control says I'm to go pronto — sorry, Pepe, be seeing you,' he said and slammed the door.

He heard Pepe's slightly aggrieved shout of '*Adios*, Joe!' Then he was roaring down the runway towards the strip of light in the sky.

As the Dragon became airborne he let out a long breath and spoke over his shoulder.

'Well folks,' he said, 'guess we made it. You all can talk to your Uncle Joey now . . . '

* * *

In the offices of *Verdad* unusual things were happening.

So preoccupied was Martyn Barrett that even the ache of his parting from Judie was slipping into the background of his consciousness.

He knew the distinctive note of the Dragon's engines and he waited until his ears caught the sound of Joe's plane passing overhead in the night sky. He sat still for a few minutes picturing Judie and Tom up there on their way to freedom. The drone had died in the north before he stirred himself and took a small bundle of envelopes from a drawer, laid them before him on the desk and pressed the bell at his elbow.

He knew it would be Tio who would come up. Tio was the oldest employee on the paper's staff and one of the most dependable; also he was a fatalist who asked few questions.

When the old man came in Barrett said, 'Oh, Tio — how many of the staff are in the building?'

'One other besides myself — perhaps two,' Tio said, regarding Barrett placidly over his spectacles. He was in shirt-sleeves and wore a green eyeshade. 'Shall I make sure, Senor Barrett?'

'No, it doesn't matter,' Barrett told him. 'Please listen carefully, Tio. In these envelopes I've put three months' pay for every employee of *Verdad* — I want you to see they're all delivered.' He paused, then added inadequately, 'We're all going to have a holiday, Tio.'

'A holiday, Senor Barrett?' Tio said, 'Is that what I'm to tell the others?'

'That's right. I'll let all of you know later on when we'll be starting up again.'

The lined parchment face below the mop of white hair was quite inscrutable. Barrett wanted to thank him for his long and faithful service but he didn't do it because it would sound like the death-knell of *Verdad* and Barrett hoped and believed that *Verdad* would not die.

'It'll be a surprise to them, Senor Barrett,' the old man said calmly. 'As it is to me.'

'Sorry I can't explain any more at the moment, I just think it advisable to suspend publication for a while,' Barrett said edgily. He handed over the bundle of envelopes and suddenly wanted the uncomfortable interview over and done with. 'Well,' he said, 'if we're going, the sooner the better. Can you have the building cleared in ten minutes, Tio?'

'Of course,' Tio said.

But at the door he turned and came back. 'I would like to shake your hand, Senor Barrett. Whatever you have in mind, I hope it'll prosper. These are difficult times.'

He held out his thin clawlike hand and Barrett took it in his own damp one and wished more than ever that the interview were ended. He was sweating all over profusely and had had his fill of emotional leavetakings for one evening. He tried to think of something memorable to say to one who had served the paper almost since its inception, but could not. 'Let me know on the blower when you're leaving the building.'

The old man nodded and smiled and went away.

Barrett lit a cigar and looked at his watch. It was exactly fifty-three minutes since Judie had left him. He could still feel the touch of her lips on his cheek. He sat and stared at the small vase of flowers on his desk.

Presently he heard the thin whistle coming up through the blower. He lumbered across to the speaking tube and said, 'Yes?'

'I'm closing up now,' Tio's voice replied. It sounded old and tired through the tube. 'Everybody's out. Good night and good luck, Senor Barrett.'

It somehow comforted Barrett that Tio had used *buenas noches* instead of *adios*. He said, lamely repeating himself, 'I'll let you know when we're starting up again, Tio.'

He stood waiting for a few moments until he heard far below the big metal grille being pulled across. Then he went down three storeys in the lift and into the compositors' room at the rear.

On one of the racks there was a galley with a cloth tied over it. Barrett himself had tied the cloth a few days before; when the editor of *Verdad* tied a covering on anything no one else dared to remove it. Now he undid the tapes at the four corners and uncovered the galley, eyeing the type already set.

It had taken Barrett very much longer to set up the type than it would have taken one of his compositors for he did not know how to use the type-setting machines and it was many years since he had tried his hand at doing this sort of thing manually.

He picked the tray up and carried it carefully into the printing-room.

There were big rotary presses here but they required a number of men to lay on and take off and Barrett had planned it as a one-man job. So instead he went to an ancient platen machine in a corner on which *Verdad*'s first issue had been printed half a century before.

He worked in his shirtsleeves and in an hour and a half by dint of much labour and concentration he had produced a thousand single-page copies of *Verdad*, printed on one side only.

It was not a first-class job and was far from satisfying his professional standards but at least it was quite readable.

He sat down and read through the last copy with care. Although he knew the contents almost off by heart he presently began to feel a sense of excitement.

He had just produced the shortest ever edition of *Verdad*, running to only a few hundred words. These were the words:

> To the Citizens of Havamo.
>
> *Verdad* has lately been the mouthpiece of Escobar. For this shameful circumstance I, Martyn Barrett, its Editor, am solely responsible.
>
> But in this special issue, the last for some time, *Verdad* is *my* mouthpiece and mine alone. No one else has been involved in its production.
>
> In Havamo today one problem transcends all others. How can Escobar's régime be destroyed?
>
> A shooting war has been tried with tragic results. Might it not now be time to try a sort of passive war?
>
> Let me explain what I mean.
>
> So long as Escobar's Army of ten thousand well-equipped soldiers remains loyal to him so long will he be able to dominate the seven million unarmed citizens of Havamo.
>
> The Army's loyalty does not, in my opinion, spring from belief in an ideology. It is bought by high pay,

luxurious living, a constant supply of prostitutes — all of which must be paid for out of Escobar's revenue.

In this matter of revenue it seems to me that Escobar is more vulnerable than most dictators. He has no outside sources from which he can borrow, no bargaining counter whereby he can obtain credit, no means of raising a loan from his neighbours.

You, Citizens of Havamo, are his sole source of revenue.

At present you are living just above starvation level, a large part of what you produce going to the Government. Under a policy of passive resistance you would continue to live just on the right side of starvation — but nothing, *absolutely nothing*, would go to the Government.

Any surplus would be burned or otherwise destroyed.

This applies to all those things which sustain life in an Army — which feed it, clothe it, or in any way contribute to its wellbeing.

Past experience has shown that in such circumstances an Army is likely to cast aside its leader, to run amok and try to supply itself by robbery and violence and rape.

During this phase some of you would die — that is undeniable. But there could be no compromise. A little fruit, a handful of nuts hidden where only you could find them — that is what you would have to live on. For the marauding, leaderless soldier — nothing. He must find himself in a barren wilderness, faced by starvation. He must be made to remember that he is in a minority of seven hundred to one. Throughout history that is how armies have melted away.

How high the price would be it is impossible to say. But, because the core of your opposition would lie in passivity rather than activity, it is reasonable to hope that casualties would be less than in poor Garcia's rising.

How long would it take? I do not

know. I think it might be hastened by the promise of magnanimity. The ring-leaders, the murderers, would, I suppose, have to be punished. But the rest — the sheep who follow — might possibly be re-absorbed and re-civilised by the seven millions.

Lastly, there can be no certainty of victory. It has been tried before in other countries. Sometimes it has succeeded, sometimes failed. By not dissimilar methods Mahatma Gandhi kindled a torch that lit a sub-continent.

In the final analysis it is, I dare say, a matter of spiritual rather than physical endurance.

The decision is for you. What I have given here is the mere genesis of an idea; the details would have to be worked out by your leaders.

I venture to place these reflections before you, Citizens of Havamo, on the chance that some of them may not already have occurred to you.

I myself urge nothing upon you, being unfitted to take any further part. I have no qualities of leadership. I have no courage. I have only shame at having for so long debased a fine newspaper.

On behalf of *Verdad* I wish you *buena suerte*.

Martyn Barrett, Editor.

It did not read as well in print as he had hoped. For a dreadful moment the gnawing doubt returned. If he had had someone more able than himself to turn to for advice, might not this message to which he had given so much thought — about which he had even prayed — might it not be exposed as a naïve absurdity, in its different way no less fallacious than Garcia's conception?

He thrust the doubt from him. Through many heart-searchings his decision had already been made. Indeed, he was no more than fulfilling his promise to Avila . . .

He put on his jacket and tucked the thousand single sheets under his arm. They were heavy but manageable.

As he went through to the entrance hall he remembered to switch off the meters. Then he let himself out with his key and pulled the big self-locking grille after him.

It was quite dark outside, the hot velvety darkness of Havamo. He stared up into the night sky for a moment, feeling himself a mote in the vastness of creation.

The late *paseo* would be already starting in the Plaza del Castillo. He went round to the back of the building and got into his car, placing the copies of *Verdad* carefully beside him on the front seat.

He drove down to the Plaza del Castillo and stopped near Paco's and sat for a moment watching the *paseo*.

The coloured lights still hung between the orange trees but it seemed to him that much of the old verve and gaiety had gone. These were just tired subdued people wandering aimlessly in a circle not because it gave them pleasure but merely from habit.

Presently he got out and carried the printed sheets over to the statue of El Bombita and set them down on the pedestal. He experienced a moment of awkwardness now because he had not given sufficient thought to this part of the plan, assuming that people would automatically pick up a sheet out of curiosity as they passed — but nobody did.

Then he realised it simply hadn't occurred to them that the editor of *Verdad* wanted to do anything so improbable as hand out free copies of his paper.

So he distributed a few sheets to those nearest him and after that it was easy. Finally he called out, 'Help yourselves, everybody — please, *amigos*, help yourselves!' and went back and sat in his car and watched the people converging towards the statue from all parts of the square.

Presently he imagined he could detect a new quality of tension in the air. And then he realised that it wasn't imagination — there really was an aura of excitement emanating from all the people who were standing in the square reading.

He knew then that his message would spread throughout Real Barba within an hour, and within a day throughout all Havamo.

He was afraid the people would come crowding round him and did not want that because he had nothing more to offer them except what was in the article. So he went back to the flat and lit a cigar and waited.

Maria brought him a cup of coffee and placed it at his elbow but he left it untouched.

He thought it unlikely the soldiers would come for him before morning. His chances of survival he estimated at about fifty-fifty. He put it as high as that only because he had a lingering hope that the elimination of an Englishman must still present itself to Escobar as a slightly more complicated operation than doing away with a *peon*.

The cold finger of fear was really beginning to touch Barrett now, but he had expected that.

He looked at his watch and saw it was almost exactly three and a half hours since Judie had said good-bye, up there in the *Verdad* office. She and Tom should be nearing Ciudad Victoria by now, perhaps had already landed . . .

⋆ ⋆ ⋆

The Dragon had been flying steadily for something less than a third of the distance to Ciudad Victoria when the port engine began to miss in real earnest.

Listening to it Joe Peters found himself sitting in a bath of sweat. He knew by instinct that the engine was going to die on him. He also knew that the Dragon could keep going precariously for a while on one motor but would progressively lose altitude.

He cursed himself inwardly for not heeding the warning signs before take-off. Ordinarily he would have investigated the trouble with all the thoroughness of an experienced flyer but in the peculiar circumstances of his departure he had viewed it almost as a blessing.

He had been chatting over his shoulder with Judie and Tom but now he clamped down on that and thought furiously how he could save the lives of his passengers and himself.

He gave himself about two minutes to decide and in the meantime lifted the plane from ten thousand feet to twelve thousand while the going was good and she would still respond.

They were over the Gulf and the Dragon was not the sort of craft that would float for more than a few minutes if he dunked her. Ciudad Victoria was quite a bit over three hundred miles ahead — two good flying hours away with both engines working normally in the slight head wind. If the port kept going even at half cock he reckoned he might get back to Real Barba in fifty minutes with the aid of the tail wind.

Those were the only two real alternatives.

If the dicky engine petered out within the next half hour the three of them would be drowned in the Gulf. That was a dead certainty — with the emphasis on the dead. If he could keep her up at not less than eight thousand he might conceivably drop down the last twenty minutes in a low-powered glide without hitting the floor this side of Real Barba.

Even then the landing would be a toss-up. And if they managed that alive there was still Escobar.

Mucking great lot of its, he thought.

His last crash landing had been in Korea. Damn it, he thought, why did it have to happen again at this of all moments?

Suddenly Judie spoke.

'What's wrong, Joe?' she asked quietly.

'Bloody port engine's not too good,' he told her. And then he decided on frankness. He knew it would be no use trying to fool this girl — she was too sharp for that. He crooked a thumb over his shoulder as if begging a ride. 'Got to go back to Real Barba — sorry, kids, it's our only chance.'

Tom whistled softly but Judie remained silent. Then she asked calmly, 'Is it going to be all right, Joe?'

'Can't say,' he admitted.

'Do what you've got to do, Joe,' she said, 'you know best. Anyway I've had a feeling for the last ten minutes Martyn needs us.'

Now that he had made his decision Joe felt a mite better. As he banked the Dragon round in the night sky he thought with grim humour, it doesn't matter so much what happens to bums like Tom and me but I'd sure dislike to kill that girl.

Like a doctor at the bedside of a patient approaching the crisis of illness he began his fight to keep the port engine alive.

He throttled down on it and pushed the good propeller control forward until the surge of power from the starboard engine threatened a pronounced drift in direction.

It was a matter of balancing a dozen things against each other until he found the nice point where least strain was taken by the sick engine. He thought twelve thousand feet was about right — for as long as he could hold it. Higher than that would need more power and there would be a loss of tail wind, lower would bring him nearer to the sickening moment when he must hit land or water.

He reckoned he had to trade everything

for maximum range.

He thought of getting Tom to jettison the mattress and the two cases but decided against it; the difference of sixty or seventy pounds probably wouldn't add up to a dozen feet of altitude.

Presently Tom crept forward and spoke in his ear.

'Look, Joe,' he said, 'any objections if I pinch your life-jacket and fit it on Judie?'

'None,' Joe told him grimly. 'Trouble is we don't carry one — my fault for skipping the rules.' He managed to grin. 'You're not flying Panam, buddy.'

Tom grinned back at him.

'Don't rub it in, Joe.'

'How's she taking it?' Joe asked.

'Oh that girl's all right,' Tom said and crept back to the mattress.

By the clock on the panel it was seven minutes after the Dragon had turned round that she began to lose altitude. This was the Rubicon Joe had dreaded. She was settling down on her final descent tangent.

During the next three minutes the Dragon fell nearly a thousand feet. Twelve minutes after the turn-round she was at ten thousand and still dropping. Now the big Texan was reduced to a hopeless consideration of the best angle at which to hit the waters of the Gulf.

And then, with the inexplicable fickleness of all fast-moving metal and against all the rules, the port engine struck an even patch. For ten blessed minutes the plane held its level and Joe began to hope again.

Half an hour after heading back the Dragon was still at eight thousand three hundred feet but had settled into a steady if slow death-glide.

Joe spoke over his shoulder to the two silent passengers behind. 'Maybe can do,' he said.

But the next twenty minutes proved to be almost the worst of all. He kept his eyes glued to the illuminated dials which now predicted that the descent tangent would join the earth just about the near rim of the airfield . . .

When he saw the lights of the runway he was coming in at ninety feet and the thing was still possible.

He sheered away from the strip and brought her parallel with the just visible line of trees. She was flying unusually silently on her one and an eighth engines. There was no sign of life in the control tower — evidently nothing was expected in, least of all the Dragon.

This side of the 'drome was pitch black and Joe did the last four hundred yards stone blind.

'Do it on your own, you bitch,' he whispered. 'Yippee . . . '

As the port engine finally died there was the padded crunch of tyres against tarmac and the Dragon shuddered and slewed and came to rest, her exit door facing the control tower.

Joe left his seat at speed and released the catch; there was no time to let down the ladder.

'Grab your bags and run like hell,' he snapped.

As she jumped Judie found time to peck at his cheek. 'Thanks, Joe,' she whispered. 'You did fine.'

By the time the searchlight came on Judie and Tom had vanished through the trees. Joe remembered the bottle of whisky in the rack above the door and reached up for it.

He was climbing leisurely out of the cabin before the three guards reached him, running full pelt from the sheds with their rifles at the ready. The foremost was Pepe.

Pepe's face eased when he recognised the contractor's pilot. He panted to a halt and let his steel-shod butt clatter to the ground.

'Joe!' he exclaimed. 'Why — what happened, Joe?'

'Her cough got worse,' Joe said grinning. 'Catch!'

He tossed the bottle to Pepe who caught it singlehanded.

'*Grazias, amigo mio*,' the guard said, grinning back. 'But why didn't you use the runway?'

'Question wasn't where,' Joe said, 'but how — in one piece or a million. Can't pick and choose on one engine, Pepe boy.'

'Go in and rest, Joe,' Pepe said sympathetically, 'while we search your plane.'

'Getting bloody regimental all of a sudden, aren't we?' Joe grumbled.

'Just had a ring from O.E. to tighten up on security,' Pepe explained. 'Search all planes out or in from now on, that's the order. Something must have happened in town, Joe.'

'She's all yours,' Joe said and strolled whistling towards the lounge.

* * *

Tom hailed a taxi a quarter of a mile from the aerodrome and they drove first to the *Verdad* offices. Finding them shut he told the driver to go on to the flat.

From the taxi they noticed little clusters of people standing about in the sultry night at corners and under street lamps, reading and whispering together.

As they drove down the hill towards the Plaza del Castillo Judie suddenly put her hand in Tom's. Usually that meant she wanted a caress. He turned towards her to take her in his arms and kiss her, then he saw the look on her face. It was unmistakably fear and he asked quickly, 'What's wrong?'

'I don't know,' she breathed, 'but something's happened. Oh Tom, can't you feel it? The atmosphere — the people out there — everything's *different* — '

He drew her close and kissed her on the mouth.

'You're tired, darling,' he said. 'It's just the reaction.'

For once she was unresponsive, cutting the kiss short. And then, as if some sort of telepathic message had flashed through to her, she said, 'It's Martyn — that's it, he's defied Escobar! I don't know how — but whatever he's done he's done openly. Everybody knows about it except us. Oh God, I should have guessed — '

Tom laughed and took her by the shoulders and shook her gently in the darkness of the taxi.

'I've heard of woman's intuition,' he said, 'but really — '

And then he noticed that the glass panel between them and the driver was opening further and the driver was handing him a sheet of paper. The man said over his shoulder, 'You are from *Verdad*, Senor?'

'Yes,' Tom told him, not really surprised that the driver should have recognised him.

'Yet you haven't heard,' the driver said. 'So it's true what he says there — he did it by himself. He's a very brave *hombre*, that Senor Barrett. I think maybe he may even put a little bravery into the rest of us.'

Wonderingly Tom took the sheet of paper and by the flashing of the street lamps he and Judie skimmed through the shortest-ever edition of *Verdad*. And when they had finished Judie clung to him and sobbed her heart out.

'Oh Tom,' she whispered, 'they'll kill him! He hasn't a chance — '

'They'll have to catch him first,' Tom said.

'He won't run away,' she cried almost angrily. 'Oh God, can't men understand anything about each other? He's afraid of being afraid but in reality he's got the most cold-blooded sort of courage. He'll just sit there in the flat smoking cigars and waiting until the soldiers come for him — ' Her hand went to her mouth. 'Maybe they've already arrested him — '

Tom leaned forward and asked the driver, 'How long has this been out — ?'

'Half an hour — perhaps a little more, Senor.'

'Hurry — hurry,' Tom said.

He turned to Judie and took her pale, tear-stained face between his hands and spoke to her earnestly.

'Listen, darling,' he said, 'it'll take a little while for the news to reach someone in authority — not long, but a little while. After that they'll have a pow-wow. They'll almost certainly decide first of all to tighten up their security measures at all the ports and roads and the aerodrome. They may have started on that already but it should keep them busy for most of the night. Only when they've got the exits securely stopped up will they begin to search in earnest inside. I think Martyn's safe till daylight.'

That seemed to comfort her momentarily. She held up her lips to him now and he kissed her and in the contact knew that her moment of weakness was over. She said quietly, 'Tom, it isn't just Martyn now, is it? That's why he sent us away — he knew Escobar would revenge himself on all three of us. You and I — we've only got till daylight too, haven't we?'

'Well,' Tom said, 'well — darling, the *peons* will probably help us — '

'How?'

'To escape — to hide — '

He sought for something reassuring to say and then realised she didn't need reassurance any more. There was a sort of defiant pride in her eyes.

'Of course he was right to do what he did,' she said. 'From his point of view it was just desperately bad luck the plane had to turn back, he couldn't possibly have foreseen that. But I'm glad it happened this way — I'm glad we'll be with him. We'll help each other get out of it somehow. I'm only sorry I got you into this too, Tom.'

'Sorry be damned,' Tom said and grinned. 'I got myself into it that day on the jetty when I kissed you good and hard. I wouldn't want that back.'

The taxi drew up at the block of flats and they scrambled out. There were few people about but Tom had the feeling that many eyes were on them : the street lamps, too, were like spotlights picking them out.

The driver waved away the note Tom offered and spoke from the corner of his mouth. 'Don't stand about, Senor. Whatever you do, do quickly, and may Our Lady protect you.'

He slipped in his gear and shot away like one glad to have been of service yet even gladder to have finished with it.

The lift was stationary at one of the upper floors so they ran quickly up the steps and let themselves into the flat. Maria stared at them from the kitchen and smiled a welcome, accepting their return as she accepted all unexpected happenings.

They found Martyn Barrett in the room overlooking the Everglades, doggedly smoking a cigar, an untouched cup of coffee on the arm of his chair.

He turned his head and stared at them

and his face took on a ravaged, ashen look.

'Judie!' he cried, 'Judie and Tom — oh for God's sake — !'

Judie ran over and knelt beside him and kissed him quickly.

'It's all right, Martyn. The plane broke down — we had to turn back. You don't have to explain, we know everything. All that matters now is, what do we do next?'

He was so shocked he just went on sitting there and staring at them. He was picturing Judie standing against a wall in front of a firing squad — dying because she was the daughter of a notorious traitor. The vision was so terrible that for a moment he covered his face with his hands to shut it out. But soon he sprang out of the chair and lifted Judie to her feet.

'You've got to get away, you and Tom,' he cried. 'Now — at once — there's not a moment to lose — '

'But where?' Tom asked quietly.

'The Cordilleras — the Everglades — anywhere. Disguise yourselves — keep out of sight — then when things quieten down, slip across the border. My car's at the side of the building, for heaven's sake take it and go — '

'Not unless you come too,' Judie said flatly.

That ultimatum seemed to steady Barrett. He put his hands on her shoulders and looked into her blue eyes and smiled.

'You know I can't do that — not even for you, honey,' he said gently. 'Thumb my nose at Escobar and then run away like a naughty schoolboy? You wouldn't really want it that way, would you?'

Judie exclaimed helplessly, 'Oh God help us, what are we to do — ?'

'I've told you — grab your bags and go,' Barrett said crisply. 'I leave her in your hands, Tom — '

Even as he spoke, the sound of the front door bell came through to them. They froze into silence. There was nothing to be done; the only entrance to the flat was also its one exit. They heard Maria's step in the hall — voices —

Then Maria's immense bulk was placidly filling the doorway, behind her a lean dark-moustached figure with a *poncho* over one shoulder.

'Senor Avila,' Maria announced.

'Come in, Senor,' Barrett said, holding out his hand, in his voice only the faintest trace of the relief he must have felt. 'I think you know Senor Clark — and this is my daughter Judie — '

Mateo Avila bowed gravely twice, sweeping his sombrero low, and then his black eyes went swiftly back to Barrett.

'We got your message, *Senor Caballero* — please God the torch will kindle. And now, what can I do to help? Of course, you must go into hiding. You have an hour — perhaps two with luck — '

'The important thing is to get Senor Clark and my daughter across the border,' Barrett said. 'For myself, I'll stay on here — '

Avila stared at him.

'But this is nonsense, Senor — '

'Damn it, man, I can't run away,' Barrett said stubbornly.

The other clucked his tongue in annoyance.

'What is this talk of running away?' he

asked, frowning. 'We look to you to lead us in the passive war. You've given us only the germ of a policy — there are many things you must explain. We four'll go to an outlying village where the people can be trusted and where we should be safe for a day or two while we discuss plans. That can hardly be called running away.'

Barrett stood irresolutely. 'I don't know,' he said, 'I don't know — '

Avila threw up his hands and let them fall with the eloquent gesture of a reasonable man faced with unreason.

'To write what you wrote,' he said, 'and then to sit down and wait for the soldiers — that may be brave but it isn't clever, Senor Barrett. To commit suicide merely leaves the work to others.'

They heard Barrett draw a deep breath. He seemed to make up his mind suddenly, perhaps stung by the other's rebuke.

'I warn you I'm no damn good at this sort of thing,' he said. 'But if you feel that way about it — '

'Then let's go,' Avila cut in abruptly. 'Every second is precious . . . '

7

The sergeant who some weeks ago had shot Pedro Carranza was named Camillo Hinojosa but everybody called him Sergeant Hino for short.

Allowing for his underprivileged background he wasn't really a bad fellow at heart although subject to moments of uncontrollable impulse. He had, after all, been reared in the Cantara district of Real Barba which is as wretched a slum as you will find almost anywhere.

As soon as he was able to walk and talk and find his way about the city, his father got him his first job, which was selling dirty postcards to tourists for a trifling commission.

Later on he drifted for a while into the fringes of tauromachy, becoming a *monosabio*, that is a red-shirted bull-ring attendant who does the menial jobs in the arena. His great hope was that one day he would become a fabulously-paid matador but he never developed enough grace or finesse with the cape for that though his sword work was good.

Also, of course, his birthmark was against him because the fans in general like their matadors to be good-lookers (though there are exceptions and God knows Manolete for one was no oil painting).

So in the end Hino had to be satisfied with joining up in General Escobar's Army which was just then being groomed for its coming role.

He didn't do it with any marked enthusiasm because army life had a bad reputation, but he soon found to his surprise that the new reality was far, far better than the old repute.

He was issued with two smart uniforms and comfortable underclothes, rapidly gained promotion to sergeant, was fed like a gladiator and never lacked a girl when he felt like one — which was frequently, for oddly enough his first employment had not succeeded in destroying his romantic propensities.

He was, in short, living better than any

member of his family had done since they first came to the isthmus nearly four and a half centuries before. As a consequence his loyalty to the man who provided these good things had the solid quality of self-interest.

That is not to say it was blind; indeed in Sergeant Hino's nature there was a streak of antagonism against all constituted authority. The first time he felt real doubts about Escobar's régime was when he shot Pedro Carranza. It was an inverted sort of doubt because Hino had an inverted sort of intelligence; there must be something wrong with a régime, he argued, that could make him do a thing like that. He hadn't really shot Pedro because he thought the *peon* was going to kill him with the fork, but because he was so obviously going to be a nuisance to the régime. (Also, of course, Pedro's reference to the birthmark hadn't improved his chances of longevity.)

However, when Hino got back that day to the barracks in the jeep, his officers — and in particular Lieutenant Valdes of his own company — had praised him for his initiative and consequently his doubts about himself and the régime had, for the moment, subsided.

The allegiance of this Lieutenant Valdes was of a different complexion. He came from an aristocratic, inbred family with a history of mental instability. His father had been a wealthy moneylender squeezing exorbitant interest rates from the *peons* until President Merida, in one of his drives against corruption, had closed the Valdes business down.

When Escobar came to power the house of Valdes rose again with him like a phoenix — the General didn't mind how much was squeezed from the *peons* provided the régime got its generous share. In the eyes of the Valdes family Escobar became the restorer of a wronged aristocracy, the one man able to shove the upstart *peons* back where they belonged.

Unlike Sergeant Hino, Lieutenant Valdes was not a person capable of being moved in any way by Barrett's article, except to loathing of its author.

On the evening of its publication — just about the time, in fact, that Mateo

Avila and the others were leaving Barrett's flat — Sergeant Hino was sitting in the mess with his collar unbuttoned and a glass of beer in front of him, alone and wondering with which of his panel of women he should spend the night, when Lieutenant Valdes entered abruptly with a sheet of paper in his hand.

It was seldom an officer entered the sergeants' mess. Hino noticed at once that the young lieutenant was on edge about something so he sprang smartly to his feet, buttoning his collar as he did so, and stood to attention and rapped out 'Sir?'

Lieutenant Valdes flung the sheet of paper on the table.

'Have you seen this, Sergeant?' he barked in his highpitched voice which always seemed to Hino to carry an undertone of hysteria.

'No, sir.'

'Well, read it some time,' the Lieutenant said shrilly. 'It's treason. The fact that it's also palpable nonsense doesn't absolve the author from the punishment due to traitors.'

'Who is the author, sir?' Sergeant Hino enquired, touching his cheek. He was not as yet in the slightest degree interested.

'Senor Barrett the editor,' Valdes informed him. 'And for God's sake leave that thing on your face alone when you're addressing an officer and try to show some interest. The article says Barrett takes sole responsibility but Intelligence thinks his daughter and the assistant editor are in it, too. My orders are to send out twelve search patrols. I'm taking the trouble to brief you myself, Sergeant, because you're in charge of the likeliest area and I don't want any bungling. Call first at the *Verdad* offices and if there's nobody there, then try Barrett's flat. I'll give you a description — '

'You needn't bother, sir,' Sergeant Hino said sullenly. 'I know these three *gringos* by sight.'

He was inwardly reflecting that you could never tell where you were with these bloody officers — one moment they praised you, the next treated you like a mangy dog.

'So much the better,' Lieutenant Valdes

shrilled. 'They've probably gone into hiding. If so, for heaven's sake try to find out something useful, some hint of their whereabouts — they can't get out of the country. Patrol along the edge of the Everglades to the southern boundary, then back by the Montezuma Highway. Question as many people as you like.' He glanced at his watch. 'Be ready to go in fifteen minutes. Understood?'

'Understood, sir.'

The lieutenant turned on his heel but paused at the door.

'All three dead or alive, but preferably alive — those are your orders,' he snapped. 'Report to me personally when you get back.'

When the officer had gone Sergeant Hino relaxed and glanced at the mess room clock. It was the sort of indefinite commission he didn't like. He had, he decided, a few minutes to spare so he sat down and picked up the copy of *Verdad*.

He skimmed through it hurriedly. Before he had gone far it appeared to him odd that Lieutenant Valdes should have allowed him to read it at all.

Then he guessed that all Real Barba must be reading it and that General Escobar had no means of keeping it from the Army. In such circumstances it seemed to Sergeant Hino on second thoughts that it was an astute move on the part of the General to distribute it himself.

The first impression made on his *peon* mind was that the article constituted a greater threat to the régime than had the rising of Jose Garcia.

He touched his cheek and sat for a moment staring in front of him in the deserted mess, wondering if the present good life were really as secure and permanent as it had appeared a few minutes ago. His thought processes were in no way analytical and he came to no very firm conclusions.

Presently he folded up the copy of *Verdad*, tucked it in the breast pocket of his uniform and buttoned it down, then glanced at the clock, rose and stretched himself.

He did not look at himself in the mirror as most of the other sergeants did when going on duty.

He would, he decided, read the article more carefully later on.

* * *

Having satisfied himself that the *Verdad* building was deserted Sergeant Hino got back into the jeep and ordered the driver to go to Barrett's flat.

As they passed through the Plaza del Castillo the sergeant noticed that the square was almost deserted. The late *paseo* should still have been on for it had just turned midnight; in its place there were only small groups here and there reading newspapers.

When they reached the flat he stationed a rifleman at the entrance and went into the hall and glanced at the nameplate board which gave him Barrett's floor and number.

As he went up the stairs he loosened the flap of his revolver holster.

Maria opened the door to him. Sergeant Hino pushed past her roughly and went methodically through all the rooms which, as he had anticipated, were empty. In the lounge his nose told him cigars had recently been smoked.

When he came out to the hall again Maria's vast figure was still there, arms akimbo. He took out his revolver and dangled it in his hand suggestively but Maria continued to look unconcerned.

'Well,' Sergeant Hino said, 'where are they?'

'Where are who, soldier boy?' Maria enquired.

Sergeant Hino touched his cheek and scowled.

'You know very well who I mean, fat woman. Senor Barrett and his daughter and the daughter's man.'

'They are not in the habit of telling me where they are going, every time they go out,' Maria said.

'How long since they left?'

'A little while.'

'Was there anyone with them?'

There was an infinitesimal pause before Maria answered.

'No.'

'You're lying, fat woman.'

'Senor Barrett and his daughter and Senor Clark went out together as they often do. There was no one with them. That is all I know. Anyway, where is your search warrant?'

Sergeant Hino grinned and tapped his revolver.

'This is my search warrant. When will they be back?'

'I do not know.'

The sergeant raised his revolver slowly until it pointed at Maria's fat stomach.

'You're lying,' he said again.

Maria's face showed not the slightest change of expression. She had, in fact, no fear of Sergeant Hino. She had once had a son very like him. This son had been born with a withered arm and had died in his 'teens. She could always tell when he was bluffing; when he did anything bad he did it on the spur of the moment so that it was already done before one even suspected his intention. But when he threatened to do anything he never carried the action through.

She said calmly, 'I do not know where they went or how long they will be away.

As Senor Barrett was leaving he gave me a little housekeeping money — but he often does that, even when he expects to be back quite soon. When the money is gone, if he has not returned I shall close the flat and go back to my village and wait till he sends for me. You pretend to think I'm lying but in your heart you know very well this is the truth, soldier boy.'

Sergeant Hino eyed this stout, ugly, elderly woman stonily for a moment or two, then he put his revolver back in its holster.

'I don't think Senor Barrett is coming back,' he said more reasonably. 'But if he does and if you are here when he comes you must 'phone me at the barracks and tell me. My name is Sergeant Hinojosa. Anyone will get me.'

'I cannot do that,' Maria said. 'It is not my place. If Senor Barrett has offended the Army in any way, that's a matter between him and the Army. It's no business of mine.'

'If you do not do it,' the sergeant said sternly, 'you will be guilty of treason and liable to be shot.'

'What nonsense,' Maria exclaimed. She spoke contemptuously but did not laugh at him. 'I'm only an old housekeeper — what do I know of treason? You and your friends have already shot a thousand of our young men, is that not enough? And now, please, you must leave. I want to lock up the flat and go to bed.'

The man who had shot Pedro Carranza hesitated uncertainly and touched the birthmark on his cheek.

It puzzled him why he did not arrest this stubborn old woman and take her to the barracks for questioning. Then he recalled a sentence in Barrett's article which seemed almost to apply to himself. *He must be made to remember that he is in a minority of seven hundred to one.*

He had an odd feeling now that he was the one and this fat old woman was part of the seven hundred.

Sergeant Hino shook himself like a dog awakening from sleep.

He said briskly, 'You must 'phone the barracks. Remember, it is your duty, just as what I am doing is mine. That is all.'

Quickly, before she could answer, he marched to the door and went down the stairs to the jeep to continue this patrol which he now felt certain would achieve nothing.

Maria stared after him for a moment. It was a pity, she thought, about the birthmark — he would have been quite handsome without it.

Then she shrugged her fat shoulders, closed and barred the door and went placidly up to bed.

⋆ ⋆ ⋆

'You, Senor Barrett,' Avila said, 'can, with a little artifice, pass as one of ourselves. The right clothes and a little dye will work wonders. But Senor Clark and the Senorita — that's a *poncho* of another colour. They're too fair-haired to be disguised.'

The four of them were sitting round a table in the disused *bodega* of Las Aguilas, which is a *pueblo* about twelve miles west of Real Barba. Las Aguilas was the native village of Mateo Avila and it was here he had brought them in their flight from Escobar.

The *bodega*, which had once housed the famous Aguilas wine, was a huge cavern-like labyrinth of empty vats and barrels, a place difficult to search thoroughly without the expenditure of much time and labour. At present the only illumination in the musty vastness was a candle on the table. Bats flitted about the entrance like bits of black paper.

Martyn Barrett stirred uneasily in the gloom.

'What do you suggest, Avila?' he asked.

The lean dark *peon* stroked his moustache thoughtfully.

'They must try again to get across the border.'

'But how?'

'Through the Everglades, Senor — there's no other way. As you know, the swamps stretch for a hundred miles. But lower down they run parallel with the coast and the far end is opposite Los Rios, which is across the border — '

'God damn it,' Barrett protested,

'they'll never get through that wilderness — they're city dwellers — '

'While Escobar lives they have finished with the cities of Havamo,' Avila said with quiet realism. 'From now on there'll be patrols in every street.'

'My daughter's little more than a schoolgirl — '

'And therefore too young to die.' The *peon's* voice was grim. 'As she will assuredly do if the soldiers find her. I'll send a good man with them.'

Across the table Judie and Tom looked at each other in the dim light. Then Judie looked at Avila.

'Why can't we all stick together?' she asked.

'Because the presence of you and Senor Clark would endanger the life of your father.' Avila's voice was frank and even sympathetic but there was no mistaking the steel in it now. 'As I've said, with luck we can pass him off as one of ourselves but there wouldn't be a chance of concealing you two.'

They sat in silence, their eyes avoiding each others', and then Avila added, 'In honesty there is this to be said, Senorita Judie. We think your father can help us in the cause, but if he wishes to go with you we won't hinder him. I would still send a man to guide the three of you through the Everglades. But it's for him to say.'

Judie saw her father draw a hand across his forehead and guessed something of the conflict in his mind.

Then he said, 'Of course I should have foreseen the possibility that the plane might have to turn back. It was inexcusable I didn't wait longer before acting. But what's done can't be undone. For God's sake try to get the youngsters out, Avila. But whatever happens, I'll stay.'

'I'd like to stay too,' Tom said impulsively.

Avila glanced at him and smiled one of his rare thin-lipped smiles.

'Believe me, Senor Clark, you'll have your hands full trying to get your lady to safety.' He sat back and looked round the table with an air of finality, intent on sealing matters at the point they had now reached. 'Then that's settled — you two will go but Senor Barrett will stay. Tomorrow I'll choose a guide and we'll discuss with him the best route through the Everglades. There'll be much else to decide as well, Senor Barrett. Some time ago I and the two men who called with you after the massacre of Santa Cruz formed ourselves into an unofficial committee of three. Three men but no policy.' Suddenly his eyes shone in the candlelight. 'Today you gave us a policy. Poor Garcia is gone, but tomorrow a new Committee of Three, with you at its head, will begin to carry that policy out.'

'I'm a scribbler, not a leader of men,' Barrett said with embarrassment. 'I never envisaged this sort of role. I only hope you won't be disappointed.'

These two men, so different in every outward aspect yet destined to be linked together in the annals of Havamo, searched each other's faces for a moment in the dim light.

'I do not think so, *amigo*,' Avila said quietly. He rose abruptly, content with the day's work. 'And now we must get you bedded down for the night . . . '

* * *

It was two days later.

In the heat of the afternoon, which penetrated even into the *bodega*, the reconstituted Committee of Three was holding its first meeting. Barrett sat at the head of the table with Avila on his right and Nino Perez on his left.

Even while he sat there it still seemed unreal to Barrett, this leadership of the cabal. But he did not wish for a moment it had been otherwise. It was, he honestly believed, much the most worthwhile thing he had ever tried to do in his life.

He had been quietly studying the men beside him. Avila he felt he knew already — about him there could be no doubts. But for a while it puzzled Barrett why Avila had chosen the tall, slim Nino Perez, so much younger than either of them.

And then Perez had spoken for a few minutes, putting forward some point for discussion, and the thing was explained. It was the first time Barrett had heard him speak at any length. The humdrum point had caught and held his attention — this man was a natural demagogue such as a cause might hope to throw up once in a generation, a swayer of crowds. He might indeed prove very useful.

Not many of his former friends would have recognised Martyn Barrett now. He wore the coloured shirt, drill trousers and fibre sandals of a *peon* and looked none too clean; a folded *poncho* lay across the back of his chair and beside him on the floor sat his wide sombrero. His face and body were dyed a light walnut colour and his thinning hair, black.

The *mestiza* woman who had done this service for him with embarrassing thoroughness had suggested laughingly, viewing her handiwork, that he would have passed for the great Pancho Villa.

Thereupon it was decided to bestow the name Pancho upon him for the duration of the passive war.

The *bodega* in which they sat had once been the crypt of a church built in the golden age of Spain in the isthmus. The church had gone in the earthquake but the crypt survived. The inhabitants of Las

Aguilas had seen no incongruity in converting it to a wine store.

Later on an ineradicable blight had come on the vines and since then the *bodega* had been derelict.

Sitting far back in the interior the three men kept glancing towards the sunlit entrance sixty or seventy yards away and could instantly have seen, across the maze of broken-staved barrels, if anyone came into the *bodega*. Behind them were passages leading from the old crypt to the open air. The Committee of Three did not intend to be taken by surprise.

Judie and Tom had already gone, in company with a guide carefully chosen by Avila.

Barrett still felt emotionally shaken by the leavetaking — at the last moment Judie had broken down and clung to him tearfully. It had taken all his own fortitude to keep him from making a fool of himself in front of the others, even though he realised Avila's plan was the only feasible one.

A paternal scruple worried him, too; he wished Tom and Judie could have been married before setting out on a journey that would take days, perhaps weeks. But a wedding involving two well-known and conspicuous foreigners, no matter how quietly carried out, would certainly have brought the soldiers about their ears.

Avila, who had been eyeing him, now said gently, 'Do not think any more about your daughter, Senor Pancho. She's in capable hands and anyway there's nothing we can do at this distance to help. She has a good chance of life — better, perhaps, than we have. And now we must concentrate on the passive war.'

Barrett, stirring himself, for the moment could think only in platitudes.

'Well,' he said, 'let me emphasise again that the important thing from the very beginning is to instil a unity of purpose into the people, to make them feel they're equal partners in a crusade — '

Perez said quietly, 'In starving the Army will the people not starve themselves?'

'No,' Barrett replied, 'the people must grow enough food to keep themselves alive — but not one crumb more.

Nothing, absolutely nothing, must be left over for the Army. A little fruit, a handful of nuts — the people'll have to exist on scraps like that and hide them away where only they can find them. Remember, it isn't only growing crops — everything that would normally go to the Army will have to be destroyed, including packaged foodstuffs in the shops, even clothing. That's the very essence of the conception.' He remembered a sentence from his article and threw it in. 'In the last analysis I suppose it's a matter of spiritual endurance just as much as physical.'

'It is a process of wearing down,' Perez said. 'It will take years, perhaps many years. The people may lose heart, Senor Pancho.'

'The length of the struggle will depend on themselves,' Barrett said, getting better into his stride now. 'If they only make a seventy-five per cent effort naturally it'll be no good because the Army could live on a quarter of the present produce of Havamo without undue hardship. Even an eighty or ninety per cent response would take a long time without making the outcome certain. But if they'll give us something over ninety-five it should cut the Army's lifeline.'

Now Avila put a question.

'Even in the passive war some must die — those are your own words. How many casualties do you foresee, Senor Pancho?'

It was, of course, a thing impossible to estimate and Avila knew it.

'At best, a few dozen,' Barrett hazarded. 'At worst perhaps a hundred — or even two hundred. But really there's no telling.'

'A small price to pay for freedom,' Avila remarked, nodding. 'And now, set our feet on the path, Senor Pancho. What do we do first?'

One man's planning of a campaign can only be tentative. No one realised better than Barrett that such things cry out for development by discussion. However, Avila had asked a direct question and he must make shift to answer.

'Instead of sending a thousand men with a few rifles let us send a hundred with tongues. Nino here will train and lead them — demagogy can shape events as surely as arms. Let them visit the heads of villages, expounding, persuading, whipping up enthusiasm — and reporting back to us. Where the response falls short we must devise means to stiffen it.' In his efforts to convince the others he was now unconsciously convincing himself anew. 'We mustn't expect quick results. Perhaps our first reward will be when some day a seemingly minor mutiny breaks out in some remote unit of the Army. At that moment all our hopes will take a bound forward — even the eventual return of the oil company will become a possibility . . .'

He went on thinking aloud like this, developing his own ideas and incorporating or rejecting the suggestions of the others, refining the overall plan in the crucible of discussion for nearly three hours and in the end a projection of the passive war really began to take shape in their minds.

Each caught further fire from the others until the private doubts which had assailed them all at the beginning, and which would return in calmer moments, began to melt away.

This is the mood in which most wars begin. It does not necessarily bear any resemblance to the mood in which they end . . .

* * *

In the Office of Escobar the General was talking to one of his Staff Colonels of Intelligence.

The Colonel was a grizzled peasant, brown as a nut, who in his youth had taken the trouble to avail himself of the free education offered at the convent school. He had risen from the ranks with Escobar and the latter had learned to respect the Colonel's subtle intelligence. Now they faced each other across the desk.

'Of course this thing's patently the daydream of an unsophisticated mind,' Escobar said contemptuously, tapping the sheet of newsprint which lay in front of him. 'An economic absurdity, utterly unworkable. Agreed?'

'Agreed, sir,' the Colonel said.

'Nevertheless if the *peons* were gullible enough to take it seriously it could cause us some inconvenience. If there's the slightest sign of that happening I must be informed at once.'

'Very good, sir,' the Colonel said.

'Meantime I think we can safely assume they haven't enough backbone for this sort of sustained sacrifice.' He paused and glanced at the Colonel probingly. 'Unless you think they've unearthed a leader who might stiffen them — someone above and beyond the usual run, someone much bigger than our late lamented Jose Garcia.'

Mentally the Colonel flicked through the files in his office, thinking from long habit in terms of hardbitten men of war who could storm a barricade. When his mind's eye came to the one he was looking for a little red light registered in his brain.

'Someone like Mateo Avila, sir?' he suggested.

'Possibly — I know little about him.'

'He lives in Las Aguilas, sir, and was a

friend of the lunatic Garcia,' the Colonel explained carefully. 'Several times lately I've suspected he might be considering forming another cabal against the régime. I could lay my hands on him at any moment — '

Escobar glanced at him quickly.

'Why don't you?'

'On second thoughts I doubt if he's quite the man to lead a rising single-handed. Once it got going he might carry it on — indeed he might be just the man for that. But I don't think he could rouse the people in the early stages — he's one of themselves, they're too used to him.'

'Sometimes I think you're too subtle, Colonel. It doesn't require a fighting man to lead a passive war. We've nothing to fear from this nonsense in a physical sense — if the *peons* want to starve themselves for a while that's their business. The only danger is that it might uncover a leader capable of catching the imagination of simple minds and becoming a legend.' The General paused and then he added evenly, 'That's the sort of thing we must continually be on our guard against. Such a man, however inept militarily, can make a people less amenable to government for generations. Why not Barrett himself?'

The other sat in silence for perhaps a minute, which is an unconscionably long time when the most powerful man in a country is awaiting your reply. But Escobar made no effort to hurry him, knowing his man.

When the Colonel replied it was as one conscious of a grievous omission.

'I must confess I completely overlooked Senor Barrett, sir. I took it for granted his part began and ended with his article. Near the end of it he said something of the sort — that must have put it into my mind.'

Escobar said, his voice harder now, 'He may be persuaded otherwise. We must redouble our efforts to find that man, Colonel. And when we do, no doubt we'll also find his daughter and his assistant editor. It's vital to make an example of all three — anyone connected with the Barrett name might help to bolster up a legend.'

'I don't think you'll find them together, sir,' the Colonel said unexpectedly. Characteristically he had used the minute's pause to think a step ahead of the other.

Escobar raised his eyebrows irritably. 'Why not?'

'A moment ago when I was considering what you said, sir, it struck me Senor Barrett may already have joined forces with Avila. Physically he's rather a nondescript type who could easily be disguised as a *peon* — which incidentally would explain our failure to trace him. Also, he speaks the language like a native. But the other two — it would be almost impossible to disguise them, they're so obviously not Latins.' He decided to venture one of his rare guesses. 'It's even possible, sir, that Barrett's at Las Aguilas this very moment and the other two are making a bid to escape across the border — probably through the Everglades.'

'Then for heaven's sake go and pick Barrett up,' Escobar snapped. 'And send a patrol to scour the Everglades.'

'I'll get a patrol out at once, sir.' The Colonel hesitated. 'I'm not so sure about

Las Aguilas — it's difficult terrain. May I make a suggestion, sir?'

Escobar nodded briefly.

'A patrol would, I think, be bound to give warning of its approach, sir. The ground round the bodega's a honeycomb of passages — it's probably there he would be hiding. It might be better to play them at their own game — send in a junior officer disguised as a *peon*. If Barrett's really there we should be able to arrange something, sir. And if he's not it would save us from exposing our hand.'

'Have you anyone in mind?'

'There's a Lieutenant Valdes, sir. He's been in charge of patrols. He's very keen — he seems almost to take Barrett's article as a personal affront. I think he'd do.'

'Valdes,' Escobar repeated. He smiled thinly. 'Ah yes, I remember him. I once did something to restore his family's fortunes — it's quite an effective way to promote keenness, Colonel.'

He considered the suggestion for a moment, while his fingers beat a gentle tattoo on the desk. It was a mannerism that made the Colonel a little uneasy.

'All right,' Escobar said at length, 'handle it as you think best. But report to me daily in person.'

'Very good, sir.'

The Colonel rose.

'One moment,' Escobar said acidly. The Colonel, also knowing his man, stiffened slightly to receive the parting salvo. 'Understand, Colonel, these people must be captured. Your efforts so far have been signally unsuccessful. Even a Colonel of Intelligence can be broken.'

'Yes, sir,' the Colonel said tonelessly.

He saluted smartly and turned away. He thought, that *Verdad* article's got him more worried than he admits . . .

8

The Everglades are not a sea, because there is too much land; nor are they land because there is too much water.

They stretch along the Havamo Keys, of which they form a part, and run parallel with the coast but overlap it by many miles at either end so that both northern and southern extremities face shores beyond the borders of Havamo.

In spite of this Havamo has always claimed the whole useless, desolate stretch of swamp as her territory.

It contains unnumbered islands of solid saw-grass where the heat is merciless. Between and around them is the maze of channels that look like green-carpeted aisles, with giant vegetation meeting overhead and the surface weed so thick that one could almost walk across it without sinking.

In these aisles a milky-blue vapour rises from the rank vegetable matter and although the temperature mostly ranges between ninety and a hundred the feeling is of clinging humidity rather than heat.

Overhead buzzards circle on the look-out for snakes. The whole region teems with turtles and alligators and the marshy fringes are brightened by colonies of pink-tipped flamingoes marching and counter-marching.

There are hidden dangers everywhere, not least the quicksands of the almost unexplored inner lagoon. The odour of decay is all-pervading.

Dawn in the Everglades, before the sky above the bare islands becomes brazen, can be of breathtaking beauty.

The *peon* who was lying stretched out on the edge of one of the islands in the growing light was paying no attention to the beauty of his surroundings. He was listening for the slightest alien sound, his hands linked behind his head and a huge sun-faded sombrero tipped over his eyes.

He wore denim trousers and fibre sandals. His bare chest and arms were so deeply sunburned that he might almost have been mistaken for a negro. He was, in fact, a young *pueblo* Indian and his name was Chikota.

Tom and Judie called him Chick. He was the guide Avila had chosen to lead them through the Everglades.

Chick's native village was Las Aguilas but he was in the habit of working for short spells at the petrol stations of Real Barba. Between these spells he would leave civilisation behind him and for months at a time live rough in the depths of the Everglades. He didn't know what made him do this; his parents were dead but that wasn't the reason. He just felt more at home out in the wilds than cooped up in an adobe hut in Las Aguilas.

He was very proud that Avila had chosen him for his present mission.

A flat-bottomed dug-out was nested deep in the shorter grass where the island merged into the tangle of the swamp. Before they left, Avila had from somewhere conjured up a rifle fitted with a silencer and now it lay by the *peon*'s side. Chick could still feel the soreness of his shoulder muscles as he lay at full stretch but it was beginning to go with the constant exercise.

For two days now he had been paddling and portaging the dug-out as quickly as he knew how, aided by the less expert Tom. They had, he reckoned, covered from fifteen to twenty miles.

As he lay on his back listening and scanning the brightening swamp from below his sombrero he wondered if the pursuit had started yet and if so, had he kept his distance. No propellers, he knew, could function in this weed. His ears were cocked for the chunk of paddles and his eyes alert for a moving profile against the dawn; he was under no illusions about the task allotted him.

Nobody knows or can know the changing labyrinth of the Everglades completely, but probably Chick knew it better than anyone living.

It would soon be time for him to make breakfast. Without getting up he glanced back towards the slight rise at the centre of the island where Judie and Tom were sleeping. They didn't seem to have wakened yet. On the first night he noticed they had slept apart, spreading their blankets out about twenty yards from each other. On the second night — last night — they had begun in the same way, but later on Chick, his ears ever alert, had heard the girl get up and had watched her go over to the man and lie down beside him under his blanket.

He hadn't watched any more. He considered Tom a pretty lucky *hombre* and vowed again to himself that he would get them both safely across the border.

He got up presently, lit a very small fire and brewed tea and cooked three *tortillas* with a little turtle meat.

When breakfast was ready the man and the woman came over and greeted him like an equal as they always did and sat down beside him, the girl cross-legged in her jeans, and ate the food he had prepared.

He noticed that this morning they seemed a little shy with each other — or perhaps they were shy with him — but he knew by their eyes that both of them were happy.

'Well,' Tom said between mouthfuls of

turtle meat, 'what's it to be today, Chick? Do we carry the boat or does it carry us? Or do we stay amphibious?'

'*Quien sabe?*' Chick replied. 'These islands — they're rafts, they move. Solid ground yesterday, maybe water today. In the Everglades one cannot plan ahead — one does as nature tells one at the moment.'

Judie chuckled. Chick liked the sound of her chuckle and had come to listen for it as one might listen for a nightingale in a garden; he felt she would probably continue to chuckle even if the soldiers of Escobar should paddle into sight.

'It's true, Senora,' he said, looking up at her. 'In the cities everyone pretends to be someone else. Here we can be ourselves.'

Before he had always addressed her as Senorita. Now, quite naturally and because it seemed more fitting, he had used Senora.

Judie nodded seriously.

'Yes, Chick,' she said. 'I think a good person might be better here and a bad one worse.'

The sun was fully up now, the morning was well aired and already it was beginning to feel hot on the island. The heat was like a giant spoon gently stirring up the life of the Everglades. Somewhere out in the swamp a school of turtles rolled over with the peculiar plopping sound of bursting bubbles; further away an alligator swished his tail down on the surface weed like a muffled whip-lash.

Chick's ears subconsciously noted these sounds and a dozen others, but they were not the noises he was listening for.

By himself, of course, he could have travelled at twice the speed but in view of the fact that one of his passengers was a girl and both were novices he was not dissatisfied with their rate of progress in the past two days. He reckoned any pursuers, laden as they would be with equipment and unused to rowing in a swamp, would be unlikely to cover more than five miles to his four. That, combined with the fact that his knowledge of the Glades would enable him to steer a much straighter line than they, gave him confidence that he could stay at least a step ahead of death.

He waited patiently until Judie and Tom had finished breakfast. They had both become very suntanned in the past two days — the face of the girl made him think of the peaches of the lower Cordilleras at harvest time, when the bloom is still on them though they have attained their full ripeness. That her life had been entrusted to him seemed to Chick the most important thing that had ever happened to him.

'Please,' he said, 'we should be moving now.'

While Chick pushed out the boat they strapped their few belongings together. Then Chick and Tom each took a paddle, Tom sitting in the stern, Chick amidships and Judie in the bows.

They had found that the dug-out handled best when the bows were lifted a little above the weed. Most of the thrust came from the Indian and was a trick of timing and controlling the slant of the blade rather than power. The art of propelling a specially constructed swamp boat is not to be mastered in a matter of days. The weed acts as a brake so that the forward movement is not continuous; between each paddle stroke the boat literally becomes stationary.

In such circumstances two expert paddlers can attain a speed of two miles per hour; Chick was satisfied with half of that.

They spoke little in their slow progress through the misty channels walled with mangrove and grapevine, cypress and palmetto and cabbage palms that stuck up like feather dusters; there is an eerie quality about the green aisles of the Glades that is not conducive to conversation. They are haunted by the ghosts of Seminole Indians and armourclad Conquistadors and many another who long ago floundered through their mazes in flight or pursuit until the slime gripped and sucked them down and finally covered them for ever.

From mud flats clusters of slit-eyed alligators watched the slow progress of the dug-out. Almost under its bows a huge snake slithered through the surface weed from bank to bank. Once indeed one of the alligators slipped into the water and for fifty yards kept leisurely pace with them, its snout within a few feet of the stern. Chick made a demonstration with his paddle and it veered off, convinced that here were no easy pickings.

But mostly Chick's attention was directed further afield; he was listening for the cries of birds far in their wake that would tell him other intruders in the Everglades were following behind.

They kept going solidly for four hours and during that time had to portage the dug-out three times over solid ground. In the channels they rested for a few minutes every half hour or so, sitting in the stationary boat, arms on knees and head on arms.

The Glades are not healthy for unacclimatised people because of the constant change of temperature from the dampness of the aisles to the merciless heat of the exposed islands. As a boy Chick had himself once suffered from swamp fever and had lain prostrated for ten days in the saw-grass without food or water. The fever is seldom in itself fatal but a solitary traveller is quite likely to succumb because in his weakness he cannot even lift food to his mouth. Chick had been lucky to survive.

In mid-forenoon they stopped on one of the islands and had a light meal and rested for an hour. Chick had planned to do a total of ten hours travelling a day, four hours when they were fresh and then two more spells of three hours each, reckoning that in this way they would cover an average of ten miles a day. In the broiling heat of early afternoon they took a siesta of two or three hours, not on an island but on solid ground on the fringe of one of the channels, spreading their blankets and lying full length.

When they finally landed for the third night on a carefully selected island Chick shot a wader bird and cooked it slowly over a small fire. The meat was dark but reasonably appetising. Tom calculated that the silencer on Chick's rifle prevented the sound carrying more than a couple of hundred yards . . .

It was Tom who first noticed that Judie was ill.

He had gone down with Chick to make sure the dug-out was safely concealed. When he came back it was getting dark but even in the uncertain light he could see that Judie's face had lost all its colour, even the tan had gone.

She was lying stretched out on one of the blankets with her eyes closed. Tom knelt down beside her and she heard him and opened her eyes and smiled at him.

'What's wrong — ?' he asked.

'Suddenly, just a moment ago, I went all weak,' she told him. 'Maybe the wader bird didn't agree with me. It's nothing — don't worry, I'll be all right in the morning.'

Chick came up and stood beside them and Tom saw that his face was grave. The Indian knelt and laid his hand very gently on Judie's forehead.

'The Senora has got swamp fever,' he said.

Judie had closed her eyes again and seemed to have lost interest in what was going on around her.

Tom said in a carefully-controlled voice, 'What can we do for her?'

Chick was remembering his own ten days of weakness stretched out in the saw-grass.

'We'll boil a little water and let her sip it now and again and maybe she'll even take a mouthful of *tortilla*,' he said. 'I'll gather reeds and build a shelter over the Senora, because she'll feel ashamed of her weakness every time she wakes and it'll help if she knows the buzzards can't see her. Tomorrow I'll plant a sort of screen to make the island look less like an island.'

He saw that Tom's eyes were clouded with a great fear so he added, 'No, she won't die, Senor Tom, but she mustn't be moved — not for ten days, maybe.'

He rose and went down towards the tangle of the channel to gather stuff for the shelter.

He was really worried now, much more so than he had let Tom see. He was confident Judie wouldn't die from the swamp fever but he had a presentiment that death in another form had drawn much nearer to all of them.

Some time during the next ten days the

soldiers were bound to catch up with them . . .

* * *

Barrett's hundred men with tongues, under the leadership of Nino Perez, had duly gone forth to visit the leading *peons* in the principal towns and villages.

They were astonished at the almost universal acceptance of the doctrine they proclaimed. In the event, Nino's demagogic flair was superfluous. Partly by chance and partly by instinct Barrett's timing had been exactly right.

But something else had happened too — something Barrett was never to understand or even be fully aware of. Yet Escobar, with that insight into the common mind which all who dominate by something other than consent must possess, had foreseen the possibility.

Since the publication of his article the personal esteem in which the editor of *Verdad* had once been held had suddenly returned — and had grown a hundredfold.

This foreigner, this ungainly Englishman who, at imminent peril to himself, was to show them how to regain their freedom had almost overnight captured the affection of the *peons* of Havamo as Byron once captured Greece. Blended into Barrett's public image was, too, the conception of the father-figure.

One result was that he was safe from betrayal to his enemies. Another was that no one stopped to question if his reasoning was as admirable as his intentions. Everyone accepted that the new policy would work.

Virtually all the hundred men had to do was to appoint a day for its inception and report back to the Committee of Three . . .

One morning soon after dawn spirals of smoke began to ascend from the fields of Havamo and from patches of waste ground in the towns.

Crops had been dug up and piled into pyramids, food-stuffs collected from the shops and heaped in the squares. Even the clothing contractors to the Army had brought out their bales of olive-coloured cloth and soaked them with paraffin. Only in secret hiding places known to the *peons* were pathetically inadequate stores of necessaries held back for their own use.

As a demonstration of near-unanimity on the grand scale it was probably unique in the annals of resistance against oppression. True, here and there a few, a very few, held out against the general spirit of sacrifice, but they were roughly handled by their neighbours and their goods added to the bonfires.

In the Office of Escobar high personages quickly gathered at upper windows and gazed out at the ascending spirals of smoke. Telephone wires began to hum. From all the barracks of Havamo presently emerged fleets of lorries and light tanks which spread at speed throughout the countryside. Soon soldiers were everywhere trying vainly to beat out the flames — vainly, because the charred paraffin-soaked heaps were already beyond saving.

Left to themselves the soldiers would doubtless have dealt out mass execution against the *peons*. But their orders were explicit. For the moment there was to be no shooting.

Although Intelligence had after all failed to foretell the precise moment when the bonfires would be lit, General Escobar himself was unperturbed.

The Army stores were full. If in the distant future the worst came to the unlikely worst it would be a simple matter for the Pioneers to sow some of the seed which was always kept in reserve; many of them had been farmers and for a while could turn farmer again.

Meanwhile there was the question of the régime's riposte.

When Barrett was brought in he would of course be executed as a traitor, but in such a way as to run no risk of perpetuating a Barrett legend. His exit from life would be so arranged as to show him up in an abject and ridiculous light, possibly even including a public recantation. He must be remembered as a misguided and tragic clown instead of a martyr.

His daughter and her fiancé, on the other hand, could best be put away quietly since the public everywhere has a stupid, sentimental tendency to sympathise with young lovers.

So much Escobar had decided. Only on the question of the *peons*' punishment was he as yet undecided. Certainly something really salutary was called for. Mass executions were not the answer since they seriously diminished his ultimate labour supply — and Garcia had already diminished it by a thousand.

Something short of mass slaughter which would yet deliver an equivalent punitive punch . . . that was the ideal . . .

⋆ ⋆ ⋆

The fires were out. The *peons* of Havamo, already living on a shoe-string, were beginning to feel the pinch of near-empty stomachs.

The Committee of Three continued to send its men throughout the country, advising, taking the people's pulse, ready to encourage the discouraged. As yet they found none.

Only the Army was so far unaffected.

It was the fourth day since the Day of the Bonfires and the régime's reaction was not yet apparent. In Las Aguilas, as throughout Havamo, the *peons* squatted in patches of shade, their sombreros tipped over their eyes. There was nothing to do, no work in the fields, nothing but to wait patiently for the Army to mutiny.

The Army gave no sign of doing any such thing. Occasionally a jeep would come round and the soldiers would inspect the fields and take notes and go away again. In appearance they were as they had always been, well fed and arrogant.

For want of any better employment the *peons* began to take walks to neighbouring villages, endlessly discussing the situation with new-found companions whom they had perhaps not met more than once or twice in their whole lives. The Committee of Three kept a close watch on this development, anxious lest much inconclusive talk should disseminate a spirit of despondency.

But they soon found that the opposite was the case. No village was willing to admit to being less wholeheartedly revolutionary than its neighbour; each boasted that no matter who else gave up the struggle, it never would.

These visits were returned and in this way the former age-old exclusiveness of village life which made each *pueblo* a little world of its own cut off from contact with its neighbour, began to be broken down.

One result was that the whole of Havamo developed a unity which had formerly belonged only to each individual village. Another was that when strangers appeared in a *pueblo* they were received without suspicion where previously they would have been looked at askance.

Now even when one day a stranger appeared in the vicinity of the *bodega* no particular notice was taken of him. The *bodega* bore no visible resemblance to a revolutionary headquarters.

But then neither did the stranger bear much visible resemblance to Lieutenant Valdes.

He spoke in the accent of east Havamo and was in every way a typical *peon* except that his voice sounded shriller and more highly strung than the average.

Mateo Avila was sitting on a barrel at the entrance to the *bodega* when the stranger passed the time of day with him. Nino Perez was inside dozing on a blanket and farther back Senor Pancho smoked a cigar at a table. It was siesta hour and the heat inside and out was merciless.

'*Buenos dias, amigo*,' the stranger said shrilly. 'Is it permitted to sit a while in the shade?'

'Of course,' Avila replied. From under half-closed lids he examined the stranger with some care. 'You're from a distance?' he suggested.

The other nodded and sat his long, slim body down against the adobe wall.

'From Cuenca,' he said, naming a village a few miles to the east. He laid his sombrero on the ground beside him, then produced two cheap cheroots from the breast pocket of his shirt and offered one to Avila. It was a considerable gesture for treating had ceased since the Day of the Bonfires, nobody having enough of anything even for himself. 'My name is Tonio Madena. How are things in Las Aguilas?'

Avila accepted a light and took a slow pull.

'We survive,' he remarked.

They sat and smoked in silence. Avila had not given his name nor had the other asked. From his seat on the barrel and from the corner of his eye Avila was examining the man seated below him on the ground. The stranger looked like a *peon* all right yet not like a man of the land. His hands were too delicately formed, his voice too high-pitched.

It could not be said Avila was suspicious but his curiosity was aroused.

'What line are you in, *amigo*?' he enquired casually.

'I keep a small shop,' the self-styled Madena said. 'Cheroots, wine — things like that.' He grinned disarmingly. 'At present the shelves are bare. It wasn't the sort of shop the soldiers patronised but just the same I threw everything on the bonfire — except for a few cheroots I kept for myself. So now I've time to visit my neighbours.'

Nino, hearing the voices, rose from his mattress and came and leaned against the entrance and nodded to the stranger.

'Meet my friend Nino,' Avila said, introducing him with a jerk of the head. 'This is Tonio Madena from Cuenca.'

Madena nodded amicably to Nino and his eyes strayed beyond him to where Pancho sat inside at the table. He took out another cheroot and gave it to Nino and nodded towards the interior.

'Perhaps your other friend would like one too?' he suggested.

'He is smoking,' Nino said shortly.

They fell, then, to talking about the passive war. This somewhat eased any suspicions Avila might have had of the stranger. Everyone talked about the passive war; if the stranger had not done so it would have been evident he had some good reason for avoiding the subject.

'This Senor Barrett, our leader,' Madena said presently in pretended hero-worship, 'I've never seen him but I'd very much like to. He must be a great man.'

'Myself,' Avila remarked, 'I've seen him several times. Once I even talked with him for a few moments in some cafe or other. It was difficult to understand what he was saying, he speaks our language so badly. But undoubtedly he is a great man.'

Madena glanced at him quickly.

'You surprise me, *amigo*,' he said shrilly. 'I always understood he speaks like one of ourselves.'

From the tail of his eye Avila noticed Nino's hand make a slight movement. Nino was, he guessed, making sure his knife was where he always carried it, in the sheath at his belt. Avila did not want any unnecessary bloodshed; if the stranger should prove to be an Army spy, well, that of course would be another matter. Even then it might be preferable to try to put him off the scent.

Characteristically Avila decided to put the matter to a stark test.

'Pancho,' he called, 'stir yourself from your laziness for a moment and come and help us settle a disagreement.'

He saw Nino stare at him in shocked surprise. Then Barrett rose from the table and came slowly towards the light, slouching as a stout, lazy *peon* might slouch.

His face was brown and greasy, his clothes dirty and greasy, his hair black and greasy; indeed, grease sat on him like a hall-mark. He looked so typical a *peon* of the poorer class that even Maria herself might not have recognised him.

'*Si?*' he asked without interest.

'Pancho,' Avila said calmly, 'my friend here asserts that Senor Barrett speaks our language like a native. I say he doesn't. I seem to remember you worked for a while as janitor in the block of flats where Senor Barrett lived, before you got too lazy to do any work. How did he speak?'

It was, of course, an outrageous trial to spring suddenly on any man. But that was how Avila liked to work. In the background, should it fail, there was always the safeguard of Nino's ready knife.

Barrett for his part was by now so

much inside the skin of Pancho that he welcomed the challenge.

'Senor Barrett spoke our language like an Englishman,' he said, his own voice broad with the authentic accent of the Havamo *peon*. The brown eyes in the brown perspiring face were bovine, without guile. 'Which is to say, *amigo*, he spoke it little better than I might speak English.'

'You see?' Avila said, grinning like a man who has won a bet.

'You were right,' Madena acknowledged. 'Perhaps I'm thinking of the other two — his daughter and Senor Clark.' He glanced back to Pancho. 'Were they good linguists?'

'I don't remember ever speaking to them, so I can't tell you, *amigo* — perhaps I was before their time.' The brown eyes were still bovine. 'Anyway, the story goes that they got across the border, so they are of no interest to anyone.'

There was silence for a moment. The stranger made no remark, his eyes for a moment as bovine as Pancho's.

Presently he said, 'But Senor Barrett

himself — surely he hasn't gone? The passive war was his idea. I shouldn't like to think we'd lost our leader.'

'I'm not in his confidence,' Avila said with a touch of sarcasm, 'but I do not think he has left the country. There was a rumour he's hiding in one of the northern *pueblos*. When the right time comes no doubt he'll return.'

'It's something to look forward to,' the stranger said, dropping his eyes.

'And in the meantime, *amigo*, I suggest it would be better not to ask too many questions,' Nino added pointedly. 'For all you know I might be an Army spy — '

'I have finished my cigar,' Pancho interposed plaintively. 'Perhaps our new friend has one to spare?'

'Of course,' Madena said and handed him a cheroot. He did it as one might hand a sweet to a small boy in a company of men.

'*Gracias, amigo*,' Pancho exclaimed effusively, showing his first gleam of interest in the proceedings. He ran the cheap cheroot back and forth under his nose appreciatively. '*Muchas gracias, Senor*.'

The hour of siesta was over and the great heat a few degrees less. Presently the stranger lifted his long body from against the adobe wall, picked up his sombrero and seemed about to go, then paused and stared curiously up at the *bodega*.

'An interesting old building,' he observed. 'Do you mind if I take a look at it?'

There was an infinitesimal pause. Then Avila said genially, 'By all means — Pancho will show you round. And perhaps Nino will be good enough to escort you too.'

The three men went inside, Pancho leading, Nino bringing up the rear. Avila remained seated on his barrel thoughtfully. There was, he knew, little of an incriminating nature to be seen in the *bodega* and what little there was would not be shown to Madena. It had been a sudden cynical quirk which had made him ask Pancho to act as guide and Nino to accompany them. But it was also sound strategy — if Madena's suspicions should be aroused Nino would sense it and the stranger would never come out alive.

Presently the three emerged in amicable conversation. They all four chatted for a few last moments before Madena thanked them shrilly, bowed and went away.

They watched him go down the dusty slope in silence until he was out of earshot. There was a hint of dejection in the set of his shoulders; he walked like a man to whom time is precious and who has just wasted an hour of it.

Nino remarked, 'Maybe he was from the Secret Police. It would have been better to have given him the knife.'

'No,' Avila said. 'There'll be casualties enough in the passive war — let the other side begin them.' And then he turned and grinned at Pancho. 'One thing's certain. Whoever he is he didn't suspect Senor Pancho has enough intelligence to contribute on occasion to *Verdad*. Also, if he was searching for Senor Barrett in the *bodega* it's unlikely it will be searched again. Congratulations, *amigo* . . . '

* * *

Perhaps Joe Peters was the only person on whom the passive war was not to leave a scar.

He had managed to get the Dragon repaired and after the plane had been thoroughly searched in accordance with the Office of Escobar's latest directions, he had soared out of Havamo for good.

For a while he was conscious of regret that he hadn't been able to get Tom and Judie out. But he had genuinely done his best and the new search regulations precluded any hope of a second attempt. So Joe, who lived very much for the day, soon forgot the episode — with Joe there were always new episodes round the corner to blot out memory of the old . . .

The whole of Havamo at this moment was rather like a bullring when the sand has been sprinkled and the *paseo* of *toreros* is over and it's a few minutes after four in the afternoon and everybody is watching the gate of the *toril* for the real show to commence . . .

9

One morning shortly before noon the fleets of tanks streamed out again from all the barracks of Havamo.

They looked very pretty in the sun, rather like shining olive-green ladybirds as they spread throughout the countryside. Their crews were armed with automatic rifles and were in every case led by a lieutenant. On this occasion they ignored the towns and concentrated on the *pueblos* in the farming districts.

Las Aguilas was one of the places visited; the routine followed there by the tank commander was identical with what happened in all the other villages. Every commander had in fact been issued with a copy of the same operation order.

The *bodega* of Las Aguilas forms one side of the village square and stands on a small mound above it, although the floor of the building, as befits a crypt, is sunk slightly below the surface of the mound.

The members of the Committee of Three, hearing the rumble of a tank, came out on to the mound to see what was going on.

The tank swirled into the square and stopped near the centre, leaving a trail of dust suspended in the air behind it. A lieutenant, a sergeant and four men climbed out; two of the men took up positions at diagonally opposite corners of the tank, their automatics at the ready. The other two quickly rigged up a loudspeaker.

Round the square the villagers were gathering in clusters, curious to hear the new line in propaganda which they expected to issue from the loudspeaker. Life had become monotonous since the commencement of the passive war and any diversion was welcome.

The lieutenant flicked his fingers across the hand microphone to see if it was alive, then held it to his mouth.

'People of Las Aguilas,' he said, and the sound of his voice carried easily over the whole village, 'gather into the square. Everyone must come — that's an Army order. You'll be allowed ten minutes in which to obey it.'

Before the ten minutes had elapsed the square was full. Everyone was there except for one or two of the very old or very ill. Avila, Pancho and Perez had come down from the mound and mingled with the crowd, which numbered perhaps a hundred and fifty.

Everybody hoped the lieutenant would say his piece quickly because there was no shade in the open square and the sun was merciless.

The lieutenant glanced at his watch and picked up the microphone.

'Who is the head man of this village?' he asked.

'I am,' Avila said.

'Your name?'

'Mateo Avila.'

'Are you satisfied, Mateo Avila, that all the inhabitants of Las Aguilas are present in the square?'

Avila glanced round the crowd.

'Except for some half dozen of the old or ill I'd say they're all here.'

'Very well,' the lieutenant said. He was

quite young but his face looked stern and his voice was as hard as steel. 'Listen carefully all of you to what I have to say. General Escobar is much displeased that you have let yourselves be fooled by an impostor who seeks only his own advancement. However the General is prepared to overlook your stupidity this time if you will give proof of repentance by returning to your fields and planting new seed. Those of you who haven't got any seed can obtain a small supply from the Army depot. People of Las Aguilas, are you prepared to give this proof? I would advise you to think well before you answer.'

The response was immediate. Everybody in the square shouted 'No!' If the lieutenant was surprised by the intensity of feeling behind the shouts he did not show it.

'Is this your final decision?' he asked calmly.

Now everybody shouted 'Yes!'

'Then you don't deserve clemency and you won't get it,' the lieutenant said. 'Nobody must leave the square until after the tank has gone.'

The tank obviously wasn't going for some time yet. The lieutenant laid the microphone down on one of the caterpillars and walked towards the crowd. The sergeant and all four men were now covering him with their automatics, their fire power more than adequate to quell any possible disturbance.

The lieutenant threaded his way through the standing people until he came to a small boy. He stopped and patted the boy's head, then took him by the hand and led him back to the tank.

The crowd watched in silence.

The officer picked up the microphone and spoke to the boy in quite a fatherly way, using the microphone so that the crowd could hear what he was saying. The boy, who was about ten years old, stood and looked up at the lieutenant without fear.

'We're going to play a game, you and I,' the lieutenant said, 'a sort of blind-man's-buff. I'm going to blindfold you and you'll walk among the crowd and touch one person and then bring that person to me. You can touch any one person you like, man or woman, anywhere in the crowd. The choice is entirely yours.'

He took a handkerchief from his pocket and tied it over the child's eyes and gave him a gentle push towards the crowd. The boy stumbled a little but sympathetic hands steadied him as he passed.

He was taking the game seriously, postponing the moment of his choice and enjoying the suspense which he could feel building up around him.

The lieutenant began to get a little impatient as the child stumbled on and on but presently the small hand went out and touched a sleeve.

'Bring forward the person you touched,' the lieutenant called.

The boy pulled the handkerchief from his eyes and took the person by the hand towards the centre of the square and when they got into the open everybody saw that he had chosen an elderly man named Pasquale, a respected and inoffensive small farmer who lived by himself.

The lieutenant dismissed the boy back to his place in the crowd and turned to the sergeant and barked an order. The sergeant propped his automatic against the tank and produced a rope and bound the old man's hands behind his back.

The lieutenant spoke to the crowd again.

'As a punishment to Las Aguilas for its disobedience,' he said, 'one of its inhabitants is about to be shot. Next week at the same time, if you still remain stubborn, two inhabitants will be shot; on the third week, three — and so on till you see reason. No one can tell beforehand who is going to be chosen. It may be any one of you who are listening to me.'

An utter silence, the hush of stupefaction, had descended upon the square. At almost the same moment, in many squares all over Havamo, a similar silence reigned. The lieutenant paused a moment to let his message sink in.

Then he said, 'Even at this last moment I will give you one more chance. Promise you will set to work in your fields tomorrow and the prisoner will go free.'

By chance in Las Aguilas the small child had chosen an old man without relatives. But in other villages the choice had fallen on a young mother or father, in some the hand of the child had even touched another child. In perhaps fifty squares people were sinking to their knees in prayer. The passive war had come to its first test.

It is on record that in Las Aguilas, as in all Havamo, no one spoke in answer to that final question.

Except Pasquale. Pasquale turned to the lieutenant and asked reasonably, 'May I say a word to them, *Senor Leftenant?*'

The lieutenant, doubtless expecting the old man to plead for his life, nodded and held the microphone to his mouth. And very distinctly Pasquale shouted into it, 'To hell with Escobar!'

After that they placed him with his back against the tank and two of the soldiers moved into position and aimed at his chest. The crowd turned away and most of the women wept quietly. A short burst of fire filled the square, causing pigeons to rise from housetops and circle for a while in the hot sky.

The murder was only bearable because

everyone was conscious that next week it might be his or her turn.

When the soldiers had dismantled the loudspeaker and the tank had rumbled away, the crowd gathered up the body of Pasquale and buried it reverently in the old crypt beneath the *bodega*.

* * *

Deep in the Everglades Tom and Chick had done their best to camouflage the island so that to anyone passing in the channel it would appear to be just a mass of tangled vegetation rising from the swamp.

It had been a big task. For two days they had pulled the longest and strongest blades of saw-grass they could find, wading deep into the channels and risking death from alligators or swamp adders.

Although the island-rafts of the Everglades are themselves composed of saw-grass it is dead stuff which has been flattened by wind or disease. The tops fall and become entangled together and welded into a solid mass; at first this mass is anchored by the roots of its constituent grasses, but gradually the roots wither because the tops cannot breathe. Then they break off and the island becomes a raft. Whether it moves or not depends on the density of the surrounding vegetation on and beneath the surface.

By its nature a saw-grass island is never covered with standing grass. What Chick and Tom had tried to do was to cover the foreshore of their island with ostensibly growing grass until it didn't look like an island any more.

Every blade that they pulled had to be stuck deep into the dead mass so that it stood upright, also the blades had to be so close together that they practically touched and planted to a thickness of some yards in order to conceal what lay behind.

They must have pulled and stuck in tens of thousands of blades. Chick calculated the screen would last for a maximum of twelve days. After that it would wither and fall and gradually become part of the raft beneath.

It was the sixth day now and Judie

showed little improvement. In her weakness she was still as helpless as a baby; Tom attended to her every need and felt no more embarrassment in doing it than a husband might feel nursing his wife.

For the first few days buzzards had hovered over the island watching them, but now the novelty of their presence had worn off and the birds had moved away. Chick was glad of this; a buzzard in the sky is like a pointing finger.

Chick himself slept very little. Even with the silencer he never used the rifle now. He was expert at killing turtles with his knife and would go foraging along the fringes of the channels to collect eggs from the nests of water fowl. He did the cooking over a tiny fire that was by some miracle smokeless, and carried the food on palm leaves to Tom and Judie. At all other times with innate delicacy he kept as far away from Judie as possible.

Judie had grown thinner; sometimes at night Tom would stare at her in the dim starlight and she looked so fragile he had difficulty in believing she could recover. People suffering from swamp fever run a consistently high temperature yet perspire profusely so that the face takes on a transparent quality and the cheek-bones are actually visible through the skin. Sometimes as Tom looked at her he found himself crying.

On the sixth night of her illness Tom, lying beside her, sensed that the crisis was at hand. Usually she was restless and her lips kept forming soundless words but now she lay absolutely still, her breathing ominously shallow. Tom spent a dreadful night, leaning on his elbow watching her helplessly. Around them the noxious swamp mist drifted close against the earth although the sky above was starlit.

Towards dawn he detected the first signs of improvement. A little colour was coming back into Judie's cheeks, the appearance of transparency was less marked, her breathing deeper. Utterly exhausted, Tom lay back and fell instantly asleep.

But in a trice he was awake again, fighting silently for breath. Against the pale dawn sky he could see Chick's head looming above him. Then he realised it was Chick's hand that was over his mouth, compelling silence. He made a sign to show Chick he understood and the Indian cautiously removed his hand and touched his own lips with a finger.

'A boat — somewhere in the channel,' Chick said in a low whisper. 'If the Senora wakes be sure she makes no noise.'

And then he was gone, vanishing like a wraith into the mist.

Tom turned quickly to Judie and saw that her eyes were open. He laid a finger on her lips; she kissed it gently and he realised the fever had gone and she had understood what Chick had said.

'Tom dear,' she whispered, 'how long have I been away from you — ?'

'This is the sixth night.'

His lips formed the words almost soundlessly but he wanted to shout with joy at her recovery.

'And because of me the soldiers have overtaken us — ?'

'Who cares about the soldiers? — all that matters is you're better — '

She put her arms round his neck and

drew his face down to hers. For a moment they forgot their imminent peril.

But suddenly from somewhere out in the swamp came the faint but unmistakable sound of paddles . . .

Down on the foreshore, peering through the screen of saw-grass, Chick was watching the approaching boat in the growing light, his rifle thrust forward.

It was a big dug-out and there were six men in it.

A sergeant sat in the bow facing forwards, an automatic rifle across his knees. There were four men in the middle, tough and fit-looking, each wielding a paddle and stripped to the waist. In the stern a lance-corporal held another automatic upright between his thighs. All the men were facing forwards except the lance-corporal who sat with his back to the others.

Near the paddlers Chick could see the barrels of four more rifles propped against the thwarts.

At sight of all that armoury Chick felt sick inside. If there had been only two armed men in the boat he might have attempted to pick them off. But the present odds would have made that suicide.

The boat was coming nearer now, seeming to ride on the low mist, and he calculated they were making nearly two miles an hour — these *hombres* were more expert swamp travellers than he had anticipated.

They must have made their night camp on a nearby island and launched the dug-out at the first streak of dawn.

The face of the sergeant was hard and keen and his eyes kept darting from side to side of the channel. It seemed to Chick that only a man who knew he was on the right scent could look as alert as that after several days of pursuit through the Glades. Chick did not flatter himself that he and Tom had left no traces when portaging through the mud flats . . .

Suddenly it seemed that the sergeant's eyes were staring straight into Chick's. For a breathless moment the Indian was sorely tempted to raise his rifle and plant a bullet plumb between those eyes — at that distance he could scarcely have missed. Then he realised the sergeant wasn't looking at him at all but was examining the saw-grass screen, perhaps struck by some unnaturalness.

The sergeant barked an order and the paddles stopped.

'That could be an island,' he said. 'Better run in and take a look — '

From the stern the lance-corporal said, 'Not with grass growing out of it, it couldn't.'

'Grass doesn't look right,' the sergeant insisted.

'Nothing looks right in the Everglades, Sergeant.'

But for long moments the sergeant continued to stare suspiciously at the wall of grass so laboriously raised by Chick and Tom. And then by some blessed quirk of Fate one of the rare, faint breezes of the swamp rippled through the screen, giving it for a moment the appearance of life and growth.

The sergeant turned away.

'Carry on, *soldados*,' he ordered, his voice edgy because he had been proved wrong and the lance-corporal right. The paddles dipped and the tableau representing imminent death began to move again against the green backcloth.

For a quarter of an hour Chick lay still until the dug-out had disappeared in the shadows of the leafy aisle and the chunk of the paddles had faded away. For the moment death had moved away but now it lay in wait between them and their goal.

The Indian continued to lie prone, thinking furiously. They could not go forward, they could not go back, they could not remain where they were.

'Chikota, *hombre*,' he murmured, addressing himself, 'it is very clear that unless we grow wings we are three exceedingly dead people . . . '

⋆ ⋆ ⋆

Of late, life seemed to have gone back on Sergeant Hino.

He had been reprimanded by Lieutenant Valdes for the failure of his patrols. The leadership of the Everglades patrol had gone to another sergeant. There had been a dozen other pinpricks — these things come in batches. The men had got to know of it as they got to know everything and he had lost caste with them.

Even his fellow-sergeants treated him with less respect these days.

Every time he was a little drunk, Hino, in the hope of re-establishing himself as the oracle of the mess, which he felt himself once to have been, had got into the ridiculous habit of pulling out the copy of *Verdad* which Lieutenant Valdes had given him and declaiming passages from it prophetically to his long-suffering messmates.

Hino's copy was by this time the only one left in the regiment — the officers had been methodically tearing up any copies they found lying about.

He varied his quotations according to the inspiration of the moment.

Usually nobody paid any attention. But now and again, when other topics were lacking, Hino did manage to attract a little notice. On these occasions it would go something like this:

' 'The Army's loyalty does not spring

from belief in an ideology — it is bought by high pay, luxurious living, a constant supply of prostitutes',' Sergeant Hino would quote pontifically. 'Right or wrong?'

Nobody would speak, so Hino would try again.

'Right,' he would answer himself, winking knowingly into space. 'That *hombre* certainly knows his stuff — you can't deny it. In the end, he says, we'll cast aside our leader and run amok — '

Here one of the senior sergeants might take notice, stir uneasily and growl a caution. 'Better be careful, Hino. That's treason — remember what happened to Ramon Garcia. They could shoot you for that.'

'They can't shoot you for reading a newspaper. Everybody in Real Barba's read it — except some of you nitwits. If it contains treason why don't they bloody well find the traitor who wrote it and shoot *him*?'

'It's not for want of trying,' someone else would remind him. 'You yourself should know that, Hino — you've been on more search patrols than anyone else.'

That being a sore point Sergeant Hino would regard the speaker with the dignity of the intoxicated; he never quite knew how to answer that one. 'Then let's confess he's too clever for all of us,' he would say, resorting to a sort of noble magnanimity. 'Maybe he's even clever enough to know which side's going to win in the long run — '

'Talk sense — how can civilians win against us? They haven't got anything. All we have to do is shoot them — '

'We've tried that,' Hino would point out. 'It doesn't seem to work — '

'It will in the end. Next time it'll be two out of every village — fifty the first time, a hundred the second. They'll soon get tired of that.'

'Maybe we'll get tired first,' Hino would suggest darkly. 'Some time the child will be bound to touch someone in our own families — '

'If that happens the officer will send him back and choose somebody else.'

'I wonder.'

'Just what would *you* do, *General* Hino?' someone would sneer.

'Try to get the *peons* back on my side — treat 'em softer, cut taxation — get them back into the fields — '

'You can't cut taxation, *estupido* — it's the only money the Government has. And you'll never get the *peons* back on your side — not after the executions — '

'Then, *hombre*,' Sergeant Hino would declare, thumping the table with one hand and touching his cheek with the other, 'I'd be damned careful not to get detailed when we shoot the next couple out of every village.' At this stage he would sometimes fall into making rash boasts. 'Or if I did get detailed I'd refuse to fire — after all we're in a minority of seven hundred to one . . . '

So the discussions would ramble on, unreasoned, naïve, stupid.

Yet without such repetitions the other-rankers of the Plaza Mayor Barracks might have forgotten Barrett's article, as their officers intended they should forget . . .

* * *

By chance Sergeant Hino *was* detailed for the next punitive patrol that visited Las Aguilas.

The villagers, with their queer *peon* pride, had held a meeting and decided there must be no evasion of attendance in the square when the tank returned. It was agreed it would be unfair for any able-bodied persons to stay away since the chance of being shot would be correspondingly increased for the remainder.

The same routine as before was followed by the patrol. The tank rumbled into the square, the loudspeaker was rigged up and the people summoned. The choice was offered and refused. The unhappy child touched two victims — this time a man and a woman — who were brought to the tank and bound.

Lieutenant Valdes, commanding the patrol, ordered Sergeant Hino to detail two men for firing duty.

And at this point Sergeant Hino (who was suffering from a slight hangover) again succumbed to one of those sudden impulses of his — the same sort of impulse, but here inverted, that had led him to shoot Pedro Carranza.

'Please, Lieutenant, I request to be excused,' he said stiffly. 'I don't feel well.'

Lieutenant Valdes turned and stared at him coldly.

'You look all right,' he said in his high-pitched voice.

'I don't feel it, sir,' the Sergeant insisted.

The Lieutenant continued to glare at Sergeant Hino, who flushed a little under the scrutiny and touched his cheek nervously. In the hot square the silence was almost a physical thing. Into the major tragedy a moment of melodrama had crept.

'You're lying, Sergeant — and for God's sake stop fingering that thing,' Lieutenant Valdes said, his lips curling — but he spoke so softly that only Hino could hear. 'You're either currying favour with the people in case they ultimately come out on top — which is stupid. Or you've been talking mutiny with your comrades and want to justify yourself in their eyes.' His hand dropped to his revolver holster and opened the flap. 'Which is it, Sergeant?'

In Hino's brain something seemed to flick back into place. It came home to him that once again he had acted too hastily. Much more preparation would be needed next time.

Characteristically Sergeant Hino, who might have brought a little distinction to a sordid episode, lowered it still further.

'It's neither, sir,' he pleaded humbly. 'I swear in the name of Our Lady I felt ill for a moment — '

Lieutenant Valdes smiled thinly. He was not without his own peculiar code of fair dealing; it might be he had misjudged his man.

'But you're all right now — ?'

'Yes, sir.'

'Prove it,' Lieutenant Valdes said shrilly. 'Instead of detailing two men you will detail one. The other will be yourself. We will give you the lady to shoot, Sergeant Hino.'

'Very good, sir.'

The moment of melodrama was over and the tragedy proceeded. The people in the square, unable to hear what had taken place, did not understand the former but well understood the latter. They turned away or knelt as the short bursts of automatic fire rang out.

Only in Las Aguilas had there been this slight hitch . . . perhaps this portent . . .

10

It was Lieutenant Valdes' turn to suffer the whiplash of authority.

In the office of the Staff Colonel of Intelligence he was being interrogated about his failure to trace Barrett.

The grizzled Colonel, himself under pressure from Escobar, was grilling his subordinate with third-degree intensity. It was he who had recommended the Lieutenant for this particular duty and that made his displeasure all the keener. The replies of Valdes had waxed shriller and shriller under the strain but the brown, subtle face opposite remained impassive and unrelenting.

Now the Colonel was probing the details of Valdes' visit to the bodega of Las Aguilas.

'How many people were in the *bodega*?'

'Two, sir — Mateo Avila and Nino Perez — '

'Anyone else?'

'No — yes.' The Lieutenant corrected himself, drawing a none too steady hand across his forehead. 'There was a third man called Pancho — a low-class *peon* of no consequence.'

'First you say two and then you say three. Now you offer an opinion when what I want is facts. Try to collect yourself, Lieutenant.'

'Yes, sir.'

'In what guise did you present yourself?'

'As Tonio Madena, a small shopkeeper from Cuenca, sir.'

'And how did you raise the subject of Senor Barrett?'

'I — I said I admired him and would like to meet him, sir. Avila replied that Senor Barrett was rumoured to be hiding in one of the northern villages.'

'I can't compliment you on the subtlety of your approach, Lieutenant. For one thing, somebody in the *bodega* might have known Cuenca well and been aware there was no such shop. Did you press Avila further?'

The Colonel's voice maintained its even, remorseless pitch. Valdes almost wished he would hector.

'No, sir. But Avila said something that surprised me. He said Barrett spoke our language so badly it was difficult to make him out.'

Now at last there was a break in the relentless questioning. The Colonel closed his eyes. He kept them closed for long moments and when he opened them again they were like gimlets.

'Was anything more said about this subject? Try to remember accurately, Lieutenant.'

'Well, sir — I told Avila I'd always understood Barrett spoke like a native. Then Avila called on one of the others to bear out what he'd said — '

'On one of the others?' the Colonel put in. 'Perhaps on this Pancho — this no-account *peon*?'

Lieutenant Valdes was getting out of his depth.

'Yes, sir — now you mention it, it *was* Pancho.'

'Go on.'

'Apparently Pancho had worked for a while as janitor in the block of flats where Senor Barrett lived. He confirmed that Barrett spoke the language very badly — like an Englishman, he said. I don't think he was trying to put me off the track, sir. He spoke quite freely and readily. I formed the opinion he was rather a stupid person, sir.' The lieutenant suddenly remembered that his opinions were not wanted and went on hurriedly. 'I said maybe I'd been thinking of the other two — Barrett's daughter and Senor Clark — and asked him if they were good linguists.'

'And were they, Lieutenant?'

'I don't know, sir. Pancho said he'd never spoken to them so couldn't express an opinion. And then he added he'd heard they'd got away across the border, sir, and so were of no further interest to anyone.'

To Valdes' surprise the Colonel seemed to ignore this last valuable piece of information.

'Describe this Pancho to me,' he said.

'He was a big man, sir, middle-aged

and rather clumsy, with thinning, very black hair. I remember he was very greasy, both in his person and clothes, sir.'

The Colonel was silent. To Valdes' surprise the inquisition seemed suddenly to have come to an end. The Colonel had closed his eyes again.

He was, in fact, reflecting with admiration on Avila's boldness in falsifying the trail; his admiration perhaps owed something to the fact that his own mind worked in very similar fashion.

He opened his eyes and fixed them on Lieutenant Valdes.

'Take fifty men to the *bodega* and arrest Senor Pancho,' he snapped. 'It's difficult terrain and the thing must be done swiftly. You're the only one of us who has seen this man, that's why I must entrust the matter to you — God knows there's no other reason. But I warn you there must be no failure this time.'

Lieutenant Valdes rose dejectedly. It seemed to him a very minor operation. He felt acutely conscious that somehow he had failed the régime to which he was so devoted.

'Very good, sir,' he said shrilly. 'I take it, then, I've been taken off the Barrett assignment?'

'Sacred Mother of God!' the Colonel exploded. 'Hasn't it dawned on you yet Pancho *is* Barrett . . . ?'

* * *

It was late afternoon in the *bodega* of Las Aguilas.

The Committee of Three were holding a meeting in the dark interior. Guards were stationed outside, sitting indolently against walls, but beneath their sombreros their eyes were alert and restless.

Pancho was depressed and worried. Not about Judie and Tom, for no news had come through of their capture and he was confident they had slipped through to freedom, but about the mounting casualties of the *peons*.

The passive war was bursting through the confines he had set for it. He was trying desperately hard not to believe that his whole conception had been a mistake. A sense of personal responsibility was eating into his soul.

In his own eyes he had become a 'scarlet major at the base, speeding glum heroes up the line to death'. For a man of his temperament it was a dreadful burden.

On the day of the second visit of the tank when the blindfold child was moving through the crowd Pancho had taken a step forward and stood in the child's path but the child brushed past him and touched someone else.

Afterwards Avila had remarked acidly, 'Don't be a fool, Senor Pancho. It is not our business to go to meet Death. Before this affair is over he will come looking for us. Meantime let us have the courage of our convictions.'

Now on this afternoon the Committee was discussing what had passed between the lieutenant and the sergeant out there in the square. There had seemed to be an altercation of some sort but none of the crowd had heard what was said.

'I saw the sergeant's face,' Nino asserted, perhaps partly to comfort Senor Pancho. 'It was incipient mutiny — and then he lost his nerve. I tell you, *amigos*, it's a good omen.'

'We are in need of good omens,' Pancho said heavily. 'Today in Havamo a hundred people died . . . '

Even as he spoke one of the guards came running into the *bodega*. Avila rounded on him quickly.

'What is it?' he asked.

'Soldiers — many soldiers in jeeps — !'

'How near?'

'At the far corner of the square they split into two columns as if to cover both entrances of the *bodega* — '

'How many jeeps?'

'Perhaps a dozen — '

Avila whistled.

'Say fifty men in all — they mean business,' he said and swung round to the heavy figure at the table. 'Go quickly, Pancho — someone may have given you away — '

'Go where?' Pancho asked. He made no move to rise.

'The sierras, the Cordilleras — anywhere. Go through one of the passages and pick up your car. Nino — go with him.'

Nino nodded but the other still hesitated.

'For God's sake go!' Avila barked, getting angry now. 'In another minute it may be too late. We'll get word to you somehow when it's safe to come back — '

Nino was on his feet. 'We'll go towards the Christ of Tlazcala,' he said with crisp decision. 'Come, Senor Pancho.'

As Avila watched them go the roar of the approaching jeeps was already filling the *bodega*.

The passages led through the old crypt to concealed exits some hundreds of yards from the building. When Spain centuries ago reared large edifices in the isthmus she not infrequently added escape tunnels if the populace was more than usually hostile.

So many of these passages exist today, they are not even pointed out to tourists. Avila judged it unlikely that the soldiers would know of the existence of these particular passages unless by ill chance some of their number should be natives of Las Aguilas.

The car which had brought them from the flat on that first night of their flight was concealed in a thicket near one of the exits. Avila hoped and believed there was a good chance it could be driven away undetected.

Suddenly the *bodega* was alive with soldiers. From one entrance a lieutenant marched briskly in with a score of men, from the other came a sergeant at the head of another score.

The lieutenant strode up to Avila. Even in the gloom Avila recognised him as the visitor of some days before who had then called himself Tonio Madena.

'Where is the man Pancho?' the lieutenant demanded shrilly.

'Pancho, Pancho?' Avila said, as if trying to fit a figure to the name. 'Ah yes, I remember now — the lazy fat one who sometimes visits us. I do not know, Lieutenant. He's a vagrant — he comes and goes like a bogus shop-keeper distributing cheap cheroots.'

Lieutenant Valdes would have dearly loved to arrest this impudent *peon*. But the Staff Colonel had forbidden it, wishing Avila left as a rallying point for the régime's enemies. When one may wish to put one's hand on a clutch of eggs at a moment's notice it is useful to know where the nest is.

Valdes wasted no words but swung away from Avila angrily and said curtly to the sergeant, 'Search!'

Avila sat quietly at the table while the soldiers turned the *bodega* inside out. It took fully half an hour; among the lumber in the place there were about a thousand empty barrels in any one of which a man might have hidden himself.

By now, Avila reflected happily, Pancho and Nino should be well on their way to the Cordilleras.

Valdes was becoming like a man demented. Already in imagination he was facing another grilling from the Staff Colonel —

But suddenly all that was changed. A soldier clattered into the *bodega*, spoke hurriedly to the sergeant, who in turn ran over to the lieutenant. Avila pricked his ears to catch the sergeant's words:

'Sir — a car with two passengers has just been seen going fast towards the mountains. It must have been hidden nearby . . . '

Fear gripped Avila. The car must have been difficult to start after its long lie-by in the open — had only now got away. He rose quickly, plucked the lieutenant's sleeve, said, 'The car has nothing to do with us, Lieutenant — '

Valdes pushed him aside, barked shrilly, 'Into the jeeps everyone — at the double!' He found time to round on Avila and spit out, 'Your turn will come, *amigo*.'

The soldiers clattered out. In a trice the vast chamber was empty. Avila was left standing helplessly by himself among the dying echoes . . .

* * *

On the powder-dry savannah track forty miles an hour was an absolute maximum. Behind them they heard the jeeps roar into movement, knew they must be clearly visible on the rising ground.

Barrett — there was no point now in the pseudonym — swung the car towards the Cordilleras with an odd feeling of contentment, almost of happiness. He was really embroiled in this thing now, where formerly he had embroiled others — the scarlet major was himself going up the line.

He took his eyes off the road for a moment to glance towards the green, humpbacked contour of the Everglades, far below and to his left. He tried to imagine Judie and Tom in some snug, comfortable room . . . perhaps Tom had already got a job and engaged the guide as a servant . . . that would be why the guide hadn't returned . . .

'Faster,' Nino urged at his elbow.

'We'll hold our distance,' Barrett said. 'Nothing can go faster on this road . . . '

They'll be married by now, he thought. Tom's a solid, dependable type, he'll look after her . . .

'There's good cover in the woods below the statue,' Nino was saying. 'When we get up there, slow down for a moment and I'll take over. Then you can slip into the trees — they won't know. Five seconds should do it — '

'And you?' Barrett asked.

'Don't worry, *amigo* — nothing'll happen to me,' Nino said and grinned fiercely. 'I know a roundabout road that leads back to Las Aguilas. Seventy-five kilometres — we'll have a pleasant trip, the soldiers and I — '

'You're sure this is best — ?'

'This is best,' the young man said.

The sun was getting low now, the boulders and shrubs on the track casting long shadows. The roar of the jeeps came up distinctly. They seemed to be about two miles behind.

Away high up the mountain to his left Barrett could see the Christ of Tlazcala on its pinnacle above the tree-line. He thought, it'll be quite an effort for a man of my age.

He had to shut everything else out of his mind now and concentrate on keeping the car on the track. Soon it would divide and the left fork would go on climbing until it petered out on the mountainside. The right was the one Nino would take. Any time after they passed the fork he must be ready to hand over the wheel and scramble out.

The slope of the cordillera was getting steeper, would soon be running on the edge of a chasm.

They were coming up to the fork now. They passed it and still Barrett did not slacken speed, awaiting his companion's word . . .

'Now!' Nino said urgently.

Barrett slowed, slipped the gear into bottom, felt Nino's foot groping for the accelerator. Then he opened the door, jumped out — stumbled, managed to keep upright —

'*Buena suerte*!' Nino called.

'Take care of yourself, Nino!' he shouted in reply.

Hidden by the car's dust he lumbered awkwardly across the track and into the trees. He heard Perez change up and roar away.

It seemed only moments until the first of the jeeps whined past. The dust had thinned and he could see the lieutenant sitting tautly beside the goggled driver. In the seat behind two soldiers gripped automatics.

Then another and another jeep whined past, bristling with armed men and driven flat out through the cloud of dust. He counted a dozen.

He had been wrong — the jeeps were certainly going faster than the car, holding the track better. The leader must be less than a mile behind and closing rapidly.

He climbed higher, keeping just inside the fringe of trees and got above the dust so he could see the road below. It had turned downwards now along the edge of the gorge, snaking among the boulders which over the years had fallen from above. It was rockier down there and there was less dust.

Barrett, measuring the gap between car and leading jeep, was dismayed to judge it now no more than half a mile.

Obviously the pursuers had no inkling that the saloon had shed one of its passengers.

Nino must have caught the image of the jeep in his mirror for suddenly he spurted to a speed far above the safety margin.

And even as Barrett watched, the unequal race came to its end. Nino hurtled towards a twist in the track, delayed his change-down a split second too long. The car entered the curve in a tail slide, almost recovered, hung for a moment on the edge of eternity, then shot out over the gorge, somersaulting again and again until it exploded into a thousand pieces among the boulders three hundred feet below. The Committee of Three had become the Committee of Two.

Stunned and sick at the death of his friend, Barrett began to run clumsily down the mountainside towards where the jeeps were congregating. The lieutenant leapt out at the spot where the tyre-marks left the track. The sound of the jeeps' engines died as they were switched off one by one.

After the roar of the pursuit the mountainside fell strangely silent.

Suddenly Barrett stopped and turned back to the shelter of the trees. Nino Perez had died in order that he, Barrett, might live. It would be poor thanks to give himself up.

It was getting dark under the trees now. Barrett suddenly felt himself very old and very useless, a false prophet foretelling liberty where there was only death.

He peered down at the distant road and saw that the lieutenant and three of the soldiers were preparing to climb down the steep slope into the gorge. He watched them disappear over the edge.

He sat down and continued to watch for an hour.

It was quite dark by then and one of the jeeps had been pushed forward to the edge and a searchlight directed from it down into the gorge. He could see little of what was happening, but presently all the lights on the jeeps were switched off and after that he could see nothing more.

He sat wondering why the lights had been turned off and then he decided the soldiers had found there was only one body in the car and had guessed that the other occupant — the one they wanted — had jumped out somewhere along the road and gone into hiding.

Obviously they were going to spread out now and search the belt of forest.

A slim crescent of a moon was appearing above the ridge, giving just enough light for a man to see his immediate surroundings and even to drive a jeep cautiously, but cutting down visibility to twenty or thirty yards. Barrett knew the lights had been put out because his pursuers did not want him to be able to pinpoint their movements.

He heard the engines start up and the jeeps begin to come back up the road. When they had got within a mile or perhaps two miles — it was impossible to judge exactly — the engines were shut off again and once more silence reigned over the whole vast slope of the cordillera.

He could not doubt that the soldiers had entered the trees somewhere below and were fanning out and upwards in search of him. Whether they would continue the search through the night or wait until morning he couldn't tell — probably they'll wait, he thought.

He groped his way deeper into the trees, sat down on a shadowy, tinder-dry log and took stock of his position.

He had no food, no weapon, not even a knife — just the greasy clothes of Pancho, the low-class *peon*.

It seemed to him that the soldiers would probably surround the mound on which stood the Christ of Tlazcala and work up towards the statue, hoping to drive him before them and out on to the bare top. If there were only fifty men the links of the encircling chain of beaters would be widely spaced at the base but would contract as the line moved up the narrowing cone.

He must therefore try to avoid being driven any higher. If he stayed where he was it might be possible to break back through a gap in the line.

With that conclusion he prepared to dig himself in for the night.

After much clumsy searching with outstretched hands in the darkness he stumbled on a hollow lined with withered moss. He felt about until he had gathered a few bone-dry branches of palmetto and Spanish ash and laid them across the top, then crawled under them and stretched himself out. He longed for a cigar but dared not smoke.

For a while he lay thinking of Judie and Tom. And then he thought of Nino Perez lying mangled there in the gorge. The dreadful feeling of personal responsibility descended on him again. Nino had joined the accusing company of all the people who had died as a consequence of his article in *Verdad*.

For one despairing moment he almost wished that he had never written it.

The forest was utterly dark now, the canopy overhead screening the moon from view, and it was very hot in the hollow. He was perspiring freely, the perspiration mixing unpleasantly with the grease which he had put on to simulate the appearance of an unwashed *peon*.

He was increasingly conscious of small aches in his legs and shoulders — the protest of middle age at having a youthful role thrust upon it. Thirst began to assail him too, without any hope of quenching it.

Outside, the night sounded to him noisier than the day. Nocturnal creatures were moving about, their soft paddings and snufflings magnified a thousandfold in his imagination. Far away the faint barking cough of a mountain puma exploded in his ears like a rifle shot.

Presently Barrett fell asleep and dreamt that he was back in the editorial chair of *Verdad* in the golden days of President Merida and that Judie was still a small girl safely at school in England . . .

When he awoke the faint light of dawn was seeping through the trees and penetrating the screen of twigs laid across the hollow. He lay for a moment wondering where he was and feeling stiff and full of aches. Then realisation came back like a great weight dumped suddenly on top of him.

Cautiously he pushed the twigs aside and raised his head.

Spears of sunlight were slanting through the tree-tops; the forest now seemed to him as quiet as a graveyard. He got up stiffly and sat on the edge of the hollow.

He felt tired and hungry and rather unwell and at a loss what to do next. He would have given a great deal for a cup of tea. And while he hesitated his ears picked up the sound of stealthy movements in the forest below.

He got up clumsily and stood behind a broad trunk and tried to scan the hillside through the screen of trees.

Three soldiers carrying rifles were coming up the slope, moving cautiously and searching the ground as they came. From above they looked like foreshortened, olive-green beetles. They were climbing in line abreast and separated from each other by not more than fifty yards; obviously they were units in a line that stretched round the cone of the mountain.

Certainly there could be no hope of breaking down past them undetected. He judged them to be about three hundred yards away or maybe three hundred and fifty. One of them was coming directly towards him and if he kept his course would have to step across the very hollow where Barrett had lain.

There was nothing left for Barrett to do but climb up the mountain ahead of them.

He turned his back on the soldiers and began the ascent, trying to keep in cover and move as silently as possible. Dead branches were heaped in windrows and he was careful not to step on these for the breaking sticks would have crackled like whips.

He went on like this for what seemed an interminable time, looking neither to right nor left but only at the ground beneath his feet and immediately in front.

When finally he paused and searched the slope behind him he still saw the soldiers through the trees.

They seemed not to have lost or gained distance in relation to himself but the spaces between them had narrowed to perhaps thirty-five or forty yards, as the cone on which they climbed had itself narrowed towards the apex.

He turned and went on again, more clumsily now because he was breathless and the muscles of his thighs were aching. Momentarily he glimpsed the outstretched arm of the Christ of Tlazcala far above him against the blue sky.

He wondered why he had been able to see it through the mass of trees and then he realised that the forest was thinning and that he had climbed through the wooded belt and would soon come out on to the bare top of the mountain.

A spasm of panic gripped and shook him; it was both terrifying and humiliating to be driven like an animal into a trap.

He steadied himself and went on again, his breath rasping painfully, until he came to the very limit of the trees. Before him stretched the bare mountain top with its stubble of yellow grass and from its crown soared the towering Christ.

For a moment in time Barrett was alone in the peace and sunlight of the summit. Far below and thirty miles away he could see the white roofs of Real Barba and over towards the east the shimmer of the Gulf. Ahead the main spine of the Cordilleras stretched into infinity. Even at that height the air was hot and motionless. There might have been no other human being within a hundred miles of that serenity.

There came a series of harsh, exultant shouts from below. The soldiers had reached the thinner belt of trees and seen him standing against the skyline.

A circle of armed men climbed into view on the perimeter of the summit, converging without haste towards the statue, sure now of their quarry, their rifles pointing to the front.

A sudden revulsion against being taken like a rodent among the trees came upon Barrett. He stepped into the open and lumbered tiredly towards the statue. When he reached the strip of shadow under the statue's outstretched arm he turned round to await the soldiers and found they had already closed the circle about him.

Oddly enough, there was no jeering from the soldiers.

Lieutenant Valdes stepped out from the

circle and walked up to him triumphantly.

'You are Martyn Barrett?' he asked shrilly.

'Yes, I'm Martyn Barrett all right.'

'By order of General Escobar I arrest you for treason,' Lieutenant Valdes said.

They handcuffed him then and led him back down the mountain towards the distant jeeps . . .

11

After much thought Chick had come to an unpleasant decision.

They must endeavour to travel the rest of the way through the Everglades without a boat.

Chick didn't delude himself about the difficulties. The odds against them all getting out alive he assessed as ten to one. But if they tried to go on by boat or return to Real Barba he put their expectation of life at precisely zero.

They had remained for ten and a half days on the island until Judie had recovered and the saw-grass screen was withering. In all they had been in the Everglades nearly a fortnight. Even if things should go miraculously well they couldn't hope to reach Los Rios in less than another fortnight.

Chick broke the news to Tom and Judie as they sat cross-legged over breakfast.

'The screen of saw-grass is dying,

amigos,' he said. 'We must go.'

Tom nodded agreement.

'I'll give you a hand to push out the boat — '

'We must go without the boat,' Chick said gently.

They stared at him in amazement. Tom said, 'But that's crazy — I don't understand — '

'*Con permisso* I will explain,' Chick said, pulling a few wisps of grass and laying them out in the shape of a fish's backbone. 'The big channel runs north and south — really it is two or three channels, not just one. The smaller ones branch out from it east and west like this, so they're no good to us. Somewhere in the big channels the soldiers are still searching. Maybe they're coming back this way. They're taking their time, making sure — you can bet they've been told to stay out there till they get us and they know for sure we can't get the boat past them in the big channels without them seeing or hearing us. So we must go some other way.'

'But what other way is there?' Judie asked.

'Through the swamp, Senora,' Chick said, looking straight into her eyes. He was still a little shy of Judie and very seldom looked her straight in the eyes. 'It'll be a little difficult because we must go as the channel goes so we don't lose direction — but about a quarter mile away from it.'

'A *little* difficult?' Tom said and laughed shortly. 'Good God, man, it's plumb impossible.'

Chick grinned at him cheerfully.

'Not impossible, Senor Tom — just difficult. We'll manage it all right, you'll see. I know the Everglades better than these dogs of soldiers. I'll scout ahead and show you the way.'

'Just how does one go through a swamp?' Judie asked quietly.

Chick shrugged, still grinning.

'As best one can. You walk, Senora. Or crawl. Or wade. Sometimes maybe you even swim. It is wonderful what one can do when there is no other way.'

'Now hold on just a minute,' Tom

protested. 'It's mud — filthy, stinking *mud*. You can't expect a girl just recovered from swamp fever to go through that.'

Chick's grin was a little forced now.

'It'll take courage. But the Senora has plenty of that, more than either of us, I think. Also, I have stayed here longer than I intended in order that she should get her strength back. I'm sorry, Senor Tom. I've given this much thought. This is the best thing we can do.'

'Can we take our knapsacks?' Judie asked. 'We've got to have something.'

Chick shook his head sorrowfully.

'It isn't possible to carry anything in the swamp, Senora — not even a rifle. We must go as we are. And soon.'

The fact that the Indian had reconciled himself to abandoning his beloved rifle was more revealing than an hour's discussion. The thing would not become easier by waiting. Judie rose to her feet.

'All right, let's go,' she said.

'*Un momento*, Senora — I'll go first,' Chick said. 'When I've gone about a hundred yards I'll signal to you to follow.

Please watch how I go and make as little noise as possible, *amigos*. That's how it will be all the way.'

And that was the full extent of their preparation for the terrible journey that lay ahead.

Chick went down to the fading screen and peered through it and listened for a moment. Then he tipped up the boat till it filled with water and sank beneath the weed. From a clump of cypress trees out in the channel a water bird squawked at him derisively.

He came back up the island and gathered up the knapsacks and blankets and dropped them into the ooze, poking them down out of sight with a stick. Then he threw the rifle after them and turned away quickly.

They followed him to the side of the island farthest from the screen and watched him lower himself into the slime. He sank at once to mid-thigh and wallowed forward with a horrible squelching sound, supporting himself by clutching at the sodden vegetation.

It seemed impossible that any human

being could force a way through the trailing fronds, mangrove roots, swamp maple and grapevine and a hundred other entanglements but he went on and on into the shadowed ways where the vegetation began to meet overhead again.

When they had almost lost sight of him he pulled himself up on a fallen and rotting log and waved to them to follow.

Judie and Tom launched themselves gingerly into the swamp holding hands but soon found it more practical to pull themselves forward by grasping at the lianas and nameless stumps that sprouted on every side.

The first impact with the mud was revolting.

It clung and clutched at their limbs obscenely and at every breaking of the surface a faint odour of decay was released. Judie sank almost to her waist and would have sunk still further had she not kept moving. She seemed to be treading on a harder under-surface of mud which yet began to yield immediately her weight was put upon it.

Her slacks felt as if they were dissolving

into pulp. She wondered how long it would be before the swamp denuded them of their clothes.

When Tom and she reached the fallen trunk they discovered that their shoes had already gone, sucked off by the bottom-mud without their knowledge.

From the waist downwards they looked like unfinished grotesques made out of some particularly unpleasant species of plasticine.

Chick grinned at them cheerfully.

'You'll get used to it, *amigos*,' he said. 'The first time is the worst.'

In one sense he was right — they did indeed get used to it as prisoners of war get used to some inhuman concentration camp. But as the hours dragged by each succeeding immersion brought a progressively crippling fatigue which paralysed their limbs.

They came to believe there was no solid land left anywhere in the world.

Mercifully on that first day they encountered no alligators, no deadly snakes, none of the killers of the Glades. There was just the mud, the foul odours, the interminable claustrophobia of the rank vegetation shutting them in on all sides.

After each follow-up they lay gasping on whatever slimy platform Chick had selected as the resting-place of the moment, and always he would grin encouragement and say, 'You're doing fine — keep going, *amigos*! Keep going!'

They had become like prehistoric monsters crawling out of the swamp, completely coated with black ooze so that only the holes which were their eyes suggested they might be human beings.

It was Chick who kept them going, Chick who climbed trees, moved ahead, paused till they caught up, moved on again, merciless and unrelenting. They almost began to hate him. They did not question how he managed to keep parallel with the distant channel. They had forgotten there ever was a channel in this world of mud. They just prayed that he would stop.

He kept them at it for two solid hours that seemed two lifetimes. Then, unbelievably, on some sort of floating haven that offered a few square yards of semi-dryness he called a halt.

'Rest here,' he said, still grinning through his mask of mud. 'Maybe I can find something to eat.'

They had stopped at one of the small channels running east and west; he disappeared, searching along the fringe.

In ten minutes he was back with a handful of berries and half a dozen small mottled eggs. They washed their hands and faces in the water of the channel. The berries were bitter but not unpleasant to the taste; Chick showed them how to make a hole in one end of the eggs and suck out the contents. It wasn't a very satisfying meal but Chick assured them he had once lived on a similar diet for weeks on end.

After that they lay stretched out on the raft for an hour, recouping some part of their lost energies.

'How many days of this do you reckon lie ahead?' Tom asked.

'*Quien sabe?*' Chick replied, shrugging, his mind running on weeks rather than days. 'I could make a guess if I knew where the soldiers were, Senor Tom. Till we find that out all is uncertain.'

They lay in silence for a while, each wrestling with his or her own unvoiced doubts. In Judie's mind the gnawing question of how Martyn was faring was uppermost, in Tom's the fear that Judie must soon collapse.

Presently Chick got to his feet and stretched himself.

'Please,' he said. 'Time to go.'

The horrible progress through the mud began again. Everything was the same — the same process of degeneration from human beings to creatures of the swamp . . .

They slept that night on a saw-grass island beside another of the east-to-west channels. Before yielding to the oblivion of the utterly exhausted they washed the outer coating of slime from their bodies in the comparatively clear water of the channel.

That first horrible day set the pattern of the week that was to follow . . . except that there were added encounters with the creatures of the swamp. But somehow

Chick's quick thinking and knowledge of the ways of the wild averted the final disaster.

They grew thinner, talked less. The slime became more difficult to wash off so that they came to look like octoroons, then darker still, like mulattos.

They moved mechanically, like something wound up in the morning, the springs uncoiling throughout the long day until petering out into complete loss of propulsive power each night.

Somehow the miracle of partially restored energy was performed anew each morning. But always the replacement was a little less than that of the day before.

To Tom it was a constant source of wonder how Judie kept going. Something was being added to his not very extensive knowledge of women without giving him an answer to the age-old conundrum how anything so vulnerable and easily hurt could yet be so tough and enduring.

In spirit they became almost indigenous to the swamp, coming in time to feel a queer affinity with the water birds that stalked among the cypress trees, the turtles that plopped in the channels — even with the alligators that watched them slit-eyed from the sick-green mud flats.

They were alternately parboiled and chilled. Their faces now were liver-coloured with fatigue, their clothes so ragged as barely to preserve the decencies — not that any of them had the energy to worry about that.

They had almost forgotten what dry land looked and felt like. Sometimes they devoured their miserable berries and raw eggs standing waist-deep in mud; on these occasions it was impossible not to eat mud too. Even on the sodden saw-grass rafts they walked with an instinctive wading motion.

And always in the background was Chick . . . Chick who covered two yards to their one, explored ahead, went off on egg and berry hunting expeditions, scouted once a day to the distant channel to keep direction and try to discover the whereabouts of the soldiers . . . Chick who grinned and urged, 'Keep going, *amigos* — keep going . . . '

On the eighth day they came to the immense central quicksands of the Everglades which stretch from the main channels to the Gulf. There is no way through them. The bones of many who have tried lie buried in their depths. It was obvious they must go round them.

Thus it became necessary for once to veer back towards the main channel.

They spent that night within twenty yards of it on a raft of saw-grass screened from anyone passing by a belt of yuccas. Chick was plainly uneasy now, so near the main artery of the Everglades. He was like a sheep-dog whose nose tells him the wolves have drawn closer.

Next morning they breakfasted on berries alone. Chick did not venture along the fringes of the channel in search of eggs. They were preparing to move forward again when they heard a distant burst of rifle fire and froze in their tracks. Chick had gone a little distance from the raft. He turned at once and came wading back to them through the dark shallows, his finger on his lips.

'Lie down!' he whispered. 'At least we

know where the *bastardos* are now — '

'What are they shooting at?' Tom asked.

Chick shrugged.

'Perhaps game. Or perhaps something moved and they fancied they'd found us. They don't mind now if we hear them — they're certain we're in the channel and can't escape them for ever. It won't occur to them we've abandoned the boat and taken to the mud. We'll beat them yet, *amigos*! And now, no more talk . . .'

They lay down behind the belt of yuccas, which the people of Havamo call the bayonets of the Everglades. In any density this grass is impenetrable to the eye.

Chick had thrown himself down at a little distance from Judie and Tom. Now he turned and whispered a last encouragement; they noticed he looked happier than for a long time past.

'When they've gone past maybe we'll be able to wade the rest of the way along the edge of the main channel. Then we could make Los Rios in four or five days from now, *gracias a Dios*!'

He touched his lips again and shook his

head and they fell silent, a new hope in their hearts.

It was almost an hour before their straining ears caught the chunk of paddles coming up the southern aisle . . .

From behind the screen they could see nothing but pictured what Chick had once seen and described — the hardfaced sergeant in the bow, the four stripped paddlers in the middle — the lance-corporal covering the rear.

It took some fifteen minutes for the dug-out to come abreast of the screen. The three listeners scarcely dared to breathe. The Everglades kept silence with them — in all the labyrinth was only the chunk of the paddles.

Then somewhere behind them an alligator stirred, perhaps nosing forward to investigate the alien sound.

The paddles stopped abruptly. A voice said harshly, 'Something moved in there, Sergeant — perhaps the *gringos* — !'

Another voice barked in sudden decision, '*Muy bien!* — give it a burst just in case — '

The Everglades erupted in a cacophony

of sound. A stream of bullets ripped through the yuccas screen. They heard the alligator flop into the channel.

The second voice said with obvious disgust, 'Bah! It's only a bloody 'gator — carry on . . .'

The echoes of the fusillade died away. The sound of the paddles started up again. Untouched by the bullets Judie and Tom grinned at each other through masks of mud. Gradually the chunk, chunk faded in the distance.

Nobody moved for a long time. Then Judie, a sudden fear clutching at her heart, crawled on her knees over to Chick.

'Chick,' she whispered, '*Chick!*'

She shook him but he made no reply.

He was lying face downwards, his forehead resting on his arms. There was something odd — something horrible — about the back of his head.

Gently she turned him over.

Tom heard her moan, 'No — oh dear God, no!' He moved quickly beside her and stopped.

Chick was lying peacefully, staring up

at them unseeingly. Between his eyes was a small hole from which blood trickled slowly . . .

* * *

Barrett was in the prison of the Plaza Mayor Barracks.

That morning the soldiers had tried to bring him in unobtrusively. But in the open jeep he had been recognised through the remnants of his disguise by many people along the route. To his surprise they had cheered him and shouted encouragement.

Now in the late evening it was oppressively hot in his cell. There were two small barred windows, one set in the door and the other in the opposite wall. Outside the door a sentry stood with fixed bayonet. Barrett got up from the bedstead and lumbered stiffly across to the window in the wall.

The barrack square was darkening. Above the machine-gun tower he could see the two skyscrapers and, a long way further off, the abandoned oil derricks.

There was nobody in sight.

Oddly enough he did not feel alone or deserted. Out there beyond the wall he sensed he had many friends. He thought, they hold no spite against me for what I've done to them.

He was very tired. He had no doubt that presently they would take him out and shoot him. He hoped it would be quick, painless. Apart from that he was not unduly apprehensive for himself, for, coming back in the jeep, he had screwed up his resolution to the point where the thought of death was not terrifying any more.

He was completely confident that Judie and Tom had got clear away. It was that confidence more than anything else that conditioned his acceptance of death.

He recalled a sentence from his last article in *Verdad*. 'Some of you will die — that is undeniable'. He had always thought of the 'you' as meaning 'us', but to print it so would have been presumptuous.

Looking out on the shadowy barrack square he thought of his long-dead wife,

Judie's mother. He did not really believe in immortality, but was not sure. It would be wonderful if he could see her again. That was one of the things he would soon know — if one knew anything. He smiled. A feeling almost of well-being came over him. Several times before in his life he had experienced the nearness of death; he recognised the peculiar state of excitement, not wholly unpleasant, which it induced.

If only there hadn't been this other thing — this massive regret filling the background of his mind. If only he hadn't miscalculated so tragically in advocating the passive war — but it was beyond him now to do anything that could redeem that. For Judie's sake it hurt him to think that his name must eventually be held in loathing by the *peons*. But it was the *peons* themselves whom he had most deeply wronged — those very *peons* who had waved encouragement as the jeep brought him in —

Suddenly there was a rattling of keys at the door and a bright light was switched on. He turned quickly. Two armed guards were standing in the doorway. One of them said brusquely, 'Come with us, *prisionero*'.

He walked between them along a corridor, up steps and then along another corridor. The iron-shod boots of the soldiers clanged metallically. He was so stiff from the previous night's exposure that he had to break into a lumbering half-run to keep up with them.

They stopped at a door, knocked, led him in. It was a bare windowless room, very brightly lit.

Seated at a table was a Staff Colonel of Intelligence whom Barrett did not know; he had hard shrewd eyes set in a grizzled peasant face brown as a nut.

'Sit down,' the Colonel said and signed to the guards to leave. Barrett sat down opposite him and waited.

There was a long pause now while the Colonel perused papers in a folder. He did not look up; Barrett began to feel a little on edge.

At last the Colonel raised his eyes.

'You are Martyn Barrett, editor of *Verdad*?'

'Yes.'

'Are you the author of the article inciting the people of Havamo to wage a passive war against the régime?'

Barrett thought for a moment of making a verbal quibble, of asking that the question be re-phrased in slightly different terms, but instead he let it go and answered again, 'Yes.'

'What you did is treason and the punishment for treason is death. Are you aware of that?'

'I know traitors are shot,' Barrett said. 'The question is whether or not I am a traitor. I suppose it depends on the point of view.'

'That has already been decided and you have been sentenced to death,' the Colonel said. 'The only question that remains is how you will die. That depends on yourself.'

Barrett said nothing. The brown face opposite was ruthless, the face of a man of war. But it was perspiring slightly, small beads dotting the forehead just below the grizzled hairline. Barrett suddenly had the odd feeling that the

Colonel was finding his task faintly distasteful.

'I should like it to be quick,' he said at last.

'We can arrange that,' the Colonel said stonily. 'But you must first do something for us.'

There was a pause. Barrett did not know exactly what would be required of him, but he knew the nature of it. It would be the measure of the difference between what is civilised and what is uncivilised.

He asked quietly, 'What must I do?'

'You must recant publicly,' the Colonel said. 'You must tell the people that what you did was dishonest and evil, that your motive was not to regain for them a liberty which they had never lost but to usurp all the power and wealth of the State into your own hands. Do this, Martyn Barrett, and I promise you your death will be quick and painless.'

Barrett sat for a while in silence.

'I'd need to think it over,' he said at length. 'I might be prepared to tell them I'd made an error of judgment, to advise them to abandon the passive war and wait for a more able leader — '

'You misunderstand me,' the Colonel interrupted. He smiled thinly, perhaps pityingly; there was a degree of naïvety in this man he had not expected. 'We do not fear the passive war — it is an absurdity, has already failed. What we want to avoid is the perpetuating of a Barrett legend. This also would carry no threat but such things have a nuisance value. They are like a small blemish on an otherwise healthy body.'

'If I am remembered at all,' Barrett said, 'it will be with loathing.'

'You must allow us to take our own precautions,' the Colonel said. 'Well, what is your answer?'

'I have wronged the people sufficiently as it is,' Barrett said quietly. 'I can't inflict on them the indignity of thinking I also made fools of them. Their sacrifices deserve something better than that — '

'Yes or no, Senor Barrett — ?'

'No,' Barrett told him. 'Of course I can't do it.'

'You absolutely refuse — ?'

'I absolutely refuse.'

'We have means to persuade you.' The Colonel closed the folder and then he looked towards Barrett but not directly at him. 'By the way, your daughter and the other two are still in the Everglades . . . '

He left the cruel sentence in the air to work its slow poison. He pressed the bell at his elbow and the two guards came in. The Colonel noted that Barrett was passing his tongue over suddenly dry lips.

'That's a lie,' Barrett said hoarsely. 'My daughter is safely out of the country — where you can't reach her — '

'You see?' the Colonel said, and in his hard eyes there was for a moment a flicker of compassion. 'You do not even know how vulnerable you are.' He nodded curtly to the guards. 'Take the prisoner away — I'll see him again tomorrow.' And then to Barrett he added, 'In the meantime I advise you to consider well all the implications.'

Barrett rose blindly and was led out of the room and back to his cell . . .

* * *

To Avila it seemed not impossible that he who had begun the passive war might now have the power to end it. He remembered Barrett's prediction that in the final analysis the outcome might prove a thing of spiritual rather than physical endurance.

Avila flogged himself to a frenzy of work, aided by the hundred men with tongues. When all else was uncertain one thing seemed certain — the people must be told. If there were to be any chance of saving Barrett's life the appeal must somehow be made on a national scale. Like wildfire the news of Barrett's imprisonment was spread throughout Havamo.

A sense of mounting climax was in the air. The knowledge, too, that within a few days three more victims in every village were to be murdered, was like a massive bulldozer pushing on events.

But Barrett himself was the centrepiece.

The horror with which the *peons* learned of the possibility of his martyrdom further increased the *mystique* and influence of his name to an extent which no man could gauge.

Of all this, as Avila well understood, Barrett knew nothing. Avila himself had only faith to throw into the scale against a mass of imponderables . . .

From all over Havamo an immense multitude began to move towards Real Barba.

They came not with any hope that unarmed numbers could storm a military barracks and rescue a prisoner — that bitter lesson had been learned. They came as vast flocks of birds congregate in an estuary, moved by some mass instinct and for some purpose which they do not fully understand. They came, too, as a sympathetic audience in a theatre, touched by what has gone before, might move in from the corridors for the final act.

They marched along the dusty roads as unemployed men march to air their grievances or the slaves marched behind Lincoln or the women of Paris on Versailles.

They came in all these moods — and in the last resort they came to mourn . . .

* * *

Next morning the Colonel of Intelligence sought an interview with General Escobar. It had been granted and now the Colonel, not without misgiving, was approaching his main theme.

'This man,' he said, 'will not serve our purpose, sir.'

Escobar regarded him coldly.

'He must be tortured then. Every man has his limit.'

'I think Barrett's limit is beyond our reach, sir,' the Colonel insisted bravely.

A gleam of contempt appeared in Escobar's eyes as he stared at the Colonel. The faces of the two became for a moment like indices of the difference in their characters, the one governed by hard rules, the other knowing no rules at all.

'I begin to doubt your zeal, Colonel. You have had one short interview with Barrett. How can you possibly measure his endurance from that?'

The Colonel said evenly, 'It's my business to deduce things from slight evidence, sir. It isn't always what a man says — sometimes what he leaves unsaid is more revealing. I've had a good deal of experience as you know — '

Escobar cut in, 'You want to be relieved of this duty, is that it?'

The Colonel stirred uneasily; he had scarcely expected to come to the kernel of the matter so soon.

'Yes, sir,' he said at length.

'Request granted. Have you anyone in mind whose powers of persuasion might be greater than your own?'

The Colonel considered. Like Pilate he had washed his hands. It would not do to wash the hands of others.

'Lieutenant Valdes might be your man, sir. He has his faults but this sort of thing might suit him.'

The Colonel remembered then that once before he had been asked a similar question and had given a similar answer.

'Very well — you may go,' Escobar said in a routine voice.

It puzzled him that this man whom he had so often used since the early days of the movement, should now for the first time be unwilling to serve him in this single respect. The difference between what he now asked and what he had asked before seemed slight.

Could it possibly be, he wondered, that there was something magnetic in Barrett's character? With that thought came the renewed determination to kill the Barrett legend before it was born.

The Colonel had risen. Escobar said softly, 'One thing before you go, Colonel. From this moment your loyalty is suspect.'

'Yes, sir,' the Colonel said.

As he went out he wondered if the time had come to try and get across the border . . .

* * *

When Barrett was led into the room for further interrogation on the following morning he was surprised to find Lieutenant Valdes waiting for him in place of the Staff Colonel of Intelligence.

Valdes eyed Barrett as he sat down and noted that he looked older, more worn.

So much the better. It really was absurd to imagine that this ungainly, paunchy, rather pathetic figure could create a legend. For once the General seemed to see a danger where none existed.

However it gave him, Valdes, a chance to bring himself to the General's notice and he intended to take it.

'Well, Senor Barrett,' he said shrilly, 'you have had a night to consider. I hope you have decided to co-operate.'

Barrett drew a hand across his forehead.

'Why don't you just shoot me and have done with it?' he said tiredly.

'You have sinned against the régime,' Valdes said. For a moment he might have been an Inquisitor lighting faggots round a stake. 'You and yours must suffer.'

Barrett looked up quickly. Here again was the dreadful imponderable that had cost him a night of agony.

He had made his decision because, no matter what the cost, it seemed to him no other was possible in a rational universe. He had hoped — perhaps doubting in his inmost heart the finality of that decision

— that if the cost were higher than he reckoned, he might never know it.

But now he must find out — he *must* know.

He said in a bleached sort of tone, 'I don't understand. You can torture me. You can kill me. But what you can do ends with me. There's nothing else.'

'You do not know? You have not been told — ?'

Lieutenant Valdes' eyes were glistening; there was in them something of the look of Garcia the fanatic. But there was also something in them that Garcia's eyes had never held.

'Told what?' Barrett asked.

'Your daughter and her two companions are trapped in the Everglades. They were attempting to escape to Los Rios — '

'But they haven't been taken? They haven't been captured — ?'

'Not yet,' Valdes admitted, his odd, inverted probity forbidding the lie direct. 'But an Army patrol has blocked the exit from the swamp. We are in constant communication with it by wireless. In a day or two — perhaps in a matter of hours — they must be caught. I give you my word this is the truth.'

'I don't believe you,' Barrett said without conviction. 'You'll never catch them — never.'

Valdes eyed him with contempt.

'Have it your own way,' he said. 'For the moment let us return to you. We are having a short speech prepared; if you'll agree to broadcast it to the people of Havamo, your desire for a quick and merciful death will be granted. You'll be executed by a firing squad and decently buried.'

'And if I refuse?'

'You will be tortured until you change your mind.'

'And if I still refuse?'

'That is unlikely.'

Barrett gave a little twisted smile.

'Humour me, Lieutenant,' he said. 'Suppose for a moment that I still won't play ball.'

'Your body, maimed from the torture, will be hung upside down in the Plaza Mayor,' Valdes said, his voice even shriller than before. It was evident the recital gave him pleasure. 'If we cannot use you for propaganda we will exhibit you as a warning. Either way you'll look pretty ridiculous. The choice is yours.'

But Barrett seemed not to have heard. He could pretend no longer; there was a question he had to ask.

'If — if you catch my daughter, what will happen to her?'

He looked of a sudden incredibly worn.

'That, too, depends on you,' Valdes said. 'If you do as we ask, your daughter will be dealt with leniently — she'll be given a short term of imprisonment and then released. But if you remain stubborn to the end, she'll be shot.'

Barrett appeared to have shrunk. Hunched in his chair he might almost have been taken for a dead man. Would it matter so much to the relatives of the hundred and fifty people who had been shot in the squares of Havamo *why* they had died? For an honourable if mistaken cause — or because a crooked Englishman had made dupes of them in an attempt to usurp Escobar's position for himself? Would it *really* matter — ?

But he could not deceive himself. Of course it mattered — mattered tremendously. These men were heroes . . . not buffoons . . .

Something in Valdes seemed to snap.

'Accept!' he screamed shrilly, banging the table with clenched fists. 'Accept! Accept!'

Barrett stirred and looked at him pityingly.

'Please send me back to my cell,' he said . . .

12

It was the following night.

The appearance of the great square in front of the barracks presented nothing unusual. It was oppressively hot and the darkness had the velvety, silvered quality peculiar to Havamo. Not many people were about. The crowd converging on the capital was drawing near but had not yet arrived. Escobar had, of course, been advised of its approach and had welcomed the news. The tableau which he was preparing would have a fitting audience.

The reports said the crowd was moving slowly and appeared peaceable. It was impossible to estimate the numbers involved but plainly they were formidable.

Presently a fatigue party with an armed escort emerged from the main gate of the barracks. They seemed to be carrying something in a sack. In the centre of the Plaza Mayor there was a magnificently ornamental lamp standard carrying a spray of high-powered neon lights; tonight it had been turned off earlier. The soldiers opened the sack and hung its contents from the standard.

When they had finished one of the party paused and looked up at the thing swinging gently overhead on its fractional arc.

'Well, anyway, he was a *hombre*,' he remarked to one of his comrades. 'Whatever they wanted him to do, he wouldn't do it. I've heard they couldn't even make him cry out when they broke his joints. By all the saints, that's the kind of courage I'd like to have.' He saluted the thing gravely. 'Rest well, Senor Caballero, wherever you have gone.'

The party returned to the barracks and the gates closed behind them . . .

Throughout the night it was evident the square was filling up with people. From inside the barracks it was impossible to see clearly what was happening in the darkness outside. As a precaution armed soldiers were stationed at all windows and artillery moved into the embrasures. But nobody felt any alarm.

When dawn broke the details gradually became clearer.

The thing hanging from the lamp standard was, of course, the inverted body of Barrett, strung up by the heels.

It was misshapen and horrible and beneath it on the pavement had formed a pool of blood which was still enlarging.

In the world of the last quarter-century such spectacles have not been uncommon. The rest of the tableau, however, *was* uncommon.

Round the corpse — not crowding upon it but at a decent distance — sat, cross-legged, a circle of mourners. Behind the nearest circle sat another — and behind it another and another and another. Like the ripples from a dropped pebble the densely packed rings went on expanding further than eye could see.

They filled the vast Plaza Mayor but that was merely the beginning.

They filled the streets radiating from it and the smaller streets that ran parallel with its sides. They filled the parks and open spaces, the alleys and forgotten corners. Where buildings intervened the human tide engulfed them, leaving them like rocks sticking out of the ocean.

Always the circular effect was preserved, as a wheel is built round the hub of its axis. This wheel covered half a city. And its hub was the hanging body of Barrett. Most of them could not even see the body but its image was passed back from mouth to mouth by those who could.

Of the seven million inhabitants of Havamo, four million were at this moment gathered in and around the Plaza Mayor. It was a vastly greater audience than the editor of *Verdad* had ever achieved during his lifetime.

When they began their journey they had not known what they would find at the end of it. If Barrett were not already dead they hoped the reproach of a vast multitude seated round his prison might gain him a reprieve. Now there was nothing for the men, women and children who composed it to do but mourn.

Some of the women were weeping, some praying. All those within sight of the body were staring at it reverently.

The strangest thing about this immense gathering was its quietness, its *pacificness* . . .

From dawn till noon the tableau persisted. No one tried to interfere with it, to change it. It was almost too big to suffer change. Even the burning sun had no visible effect.

Shortly before noon, however, came a new motif.

Out on the high balcony of the barracks stepped an armed bodyguard led by Sergeant Hino. They lined the balustrades, their rifles at the ready, leaving a path open to the microphone which stood at the front of the balcony. And presently to the microphone came Lieutenant Valdes.

It was, perhaps, odd that so junior an officer should have been selected for so important a task. Escobar himself might have come — but it is better to preserve the unapproachability of the hierarchy. Normally it would have fallen to the Staff Colonel of Intelligence — but he was unavailable.

So to Valdes — whom Escobar now had spotted as the coming man, the dedicated servitor whose loyalty would never be suspect — had fallen the honour.

He made the speech which Barrett might have made, suitably amended. He chided the people for their naïvety in allowing themselves to be misled by a scoundrel whose one ambition was to usurp the power and wealth of the State for himsef. The blame for their mistakes and miseries lay at the feet of the miserable wretch — the tragic clown — whose body hung before them.

The speaker heaped more ridicule on the ungainly, inverted corpse, essayed a joke or two at its expense, pointed at it in derision.

He finished confidently: 'The pretended modesty of his article fooled you but by now even the simplest of you must realise his true aims. He did you a great wrong. He was an evil man. Forget him. Go home quietly like sensible people and tomorrow get back to your work in the fields.'

The crowd did not move.

Lieutenant Valdes, disconcerted and a little angered, again appealed to them to go home. Still they paid no attention. They were, to tell the truth, scarcely conscious of the living figure on the balcony. It was the dead one that drew all their attention.

Others had died in the same cause — *their* cause. But this man from another land had espoused a cause not his own. He had pointed a way, served in the campaign, died hideously and lingeringly on their behalf.

Pitiable, tortured Barrett had become The Martyr.

In sudden fury Lieutenant Valdes beat with both fists on the balustrade of the balcony and screamed into the microphone, 'Go, all of you! Go home at once — or I will order the soldiers to fire a volley!'

He waited, pale and trembling, for some response but there wasn't any. Sergeant Hino, beside him on the balcony, touched his birthmark nervously.

And then Lieutenant Valdes uttered the

one word which was destined to bring the passive war to its end. The word was 'Fire!'

Again, to his horror, there was no response.

There were, perhaps, a thousand armed soldiers lining the windows and embrasures and balconies of the barracks who heard the command. Most of them had taken the events of Garcia's rising in their unthinking stride. But firing on four million people is an undertaking to make even the most unthinking think.

Will one volley be enough? If not, where will the line be drawn, where will it end? In bloodshed unspeakable? — or in a crushing of the armed by the sheer weight of numbers of the unarmed?

The anatomy of mutiny is not to be dissected neatly. The very size of the crowd, a belated recognition that the people seated quietly in the square were not enemies but their own flesh and blood — these were factors certainly. But in some odd way the life-force of the mutiny flowed from the lifeless thing suspended from the lamp standard.

Even then events might have settled back somehow into a sort of impotent stability had not a finger touched the swaying mass.

The finger was Sergeant Hino's. He was to succeed where once before he had signally failed.

Lieutenant Valdes swung round on him furiously and screeched, 'Fire, you disfigured dolt — fire!'

Sergeant Hino did indeed obey the command to fire. By one of his ungovernable impulses he discharged his rifle full in the face of Lieutenant Valdes, who crumpled and fell, his head a hideous ruin, pulling the microphone down with him.

At that moment the clock in the barracks tower began to chime the hour of noon.

The chain reaction which followed the shooting was, in all the circumstances, perhaps inevitable.

There was no cheering, no elation — the corpse of Barrett seemed to forbid it. That this was the apogee of Escobar's régime — that there could be no recovery

— was not in doubt, was accepted as something already in the past.

The soldiers laid aside their arms and from windows and embrasures began to climb down into the square and mingle with the crowd, who received them in silence.

The Headquarters of the Army of Havamo, which had repelled a thousand living men, had fallen to a dead one.

Somebody — whether a soldier or civilian is immaterial — clambered up the lamp standard and cut down the body of Barrett.

Avila signed to half a dozen men and the little group formed a wedge in the crowd and sought out Sergeant Hino, who had descended into the square with the rest of the soldiers. Avila tapped him on the shoulder and said, 'A moment, *amigo* — where can we find Escobar?'

Sergeant Hino, still a little stunned by what he had done, touched his cheek with one hand and pointed along the square with the other.

'He'll be in his room in the Office of Escobar — come, I'll show you, Senors.

He won't be able to get away because of the crowd.'

Already the barracks were deserted. The olive-green uniforms of the soldiers were becoming indistinguishable in the crowd. The body of Barrett was being borne reverently away by soldiers and civilians alike.

There was triumph as well as reverence for everyone knew that what Real Barba had done today all Havamo would do tomorrow.

Barrett's forecast of the course of the passive war had proved inaccurate. But its ending would not have disappointed him . . .

* * *

The southern tip of the Everglades peters out about a mile from the bay of Los Rios. An arm of the bay runs up for a short distance between the swamp and the mainland. The mud of the Everglades dies as it meets a sandbar stretching across the mouth of this inlet. On the fringe of the marsh pink-tipped flamingoes march and countermarch.

At low tide the crossing between the swamp and the golden bay round which the city spreads can be made on foot through the shallow water rippling over the sandbar.

Los Rios is a modern city of white skyscrapers and is situated some thirty miles beyond the borders of Havamo.

A little after noon on the day Valdes died Tom helped Judie to crawl through the last loathsome defences of the Everglades and together they gazed in wonder at the clean sunlit bay stretching before them and the soaring buildings beyond.

They were emaciated, bare-foot and in rags, covered in slime and almost at the limit of their endurance. Los Rios looked to them like a vision of the Celestial City.

They embraced and Judie wept a little. Then they went down into the warm waters of the bay and washed the mud from their bodies for the last time. For a while they sat on the foreshore and let the hot sun dry their rags. Some of their fatigue had been washed away too and they talked about Martyn whom they hoped soon to see again and about Chick whom they knew they could never see again.

After that they joined hands and waded across the sandbar towards the shining city . . .

* * *

It was a year later, the first anniversary of the Army mutiny.

There had been changes in Havamo. Avila was President; the land taken from the *peons* had been restored to them and the farms were being cultivated by their traditional owners; black bull calves, the future sires of herds, roamed the pastures of the *ganaderias*; a new lease had been granted to the oil company and it was hoped the wells would soon be back in production.

All was not yet perfect but no man slept in fear of being shot on the morrow. Some even believed an age more golden than that of Merida was on its way.

As Barrett had forecast, the majority of

the ex-soldiers of Escobar's Army had been assimilated into the civilian population. Most of the menial jobs fell to their lot but with one exception Avila had decreed against reprisals.

The one exception was General Escobar himself. On the day of the mutiny he had been dragged from his office and beaten to death on the pavement outside. A countless multitude had stamped upon his body and spat into the pulped face.

Barrett had been buried high on the Cordilleras at the spot where he had been captured near the Christ of Tlazcala. Down below in the Plaza Mayor the lamp standard from which he had hung had been taken down and a massive granite column erected in its place. It was a thing of great strength and simplicity and on it were carved the words, *In Memory of Martyn Barrett the Liberator*.

On this first anniversary the new editor of *Verdad* and his wife Judie were looking down on the Plaza Mayor from the windows of the editorial office.

Behind them Maria dandled their baby son Martyn Chikota who had been conceived in the Everglades. In the square an immense crowd, which had come from all over Havamo for the anniversary, encircled the column as a wheel encircles the hub of its axis. In the forefront facing the column stood President Avila and immediately behind him were ranged the members of his Government.

From the barracks tower a clock began to chime the hour of noon. The watchers in the window could see that all over the square sombreros were being taken off and everyone was standing bare-headed. Judie and Tom did not speak but their hands sought each other's and clasped tightly.

What Escobar most feared had already happened — Martyn Barrett had become a legend.

Behind them Maria made playful faces at Martyn Chikota. She could not help thinking it was a pity so fine a *caballero* as the child's grandfather had got himself killed in such an unimportant little affray.

After all less than two hundred people had died in the passive war — why, the earthquake had killed ten times as many as that, Garcia's rising five times as many.

Outside in the hot square all the people were still standing bareheaded and silent . . .

THE END

Other titles in the
Linford Mystery Library:

THAT INFERNAL TRIANGLE

Mark Ashton

An aeroplane goes down in the notorious Bermuda Triangle and on board is an Englishman recently heavily insured. The suspicious insurance company calls in Dan Felsen, former RAF pilot turned private investigator. Dan soon runs into trouble, which makes him suspect the infernal triangle is being used as a front for a much more sinister reason for the disappearance. His search for clues leads him to the Bahamas, the Caribbean and into a hurricane before he resolves the mystery.

THE GUILTY WITNESSES

John Newton Chance

Jonathan Blake had become involved in finding out just who had stolen a precious statuette. A gang of amateurs had so clever a plot that they had attracted the attention of a group of international spies, who habitually used amateurs as guide dogs to secret places of treasure and other things. Then, of course, the amateurs were disposed of. Jonathan Blake found himself being shot at because the guide dogs had lost their way . . .